Nine Degrees North

THE ACTIONS OF THE PAST HAVE
FOLLOWED THEM HOME

By
Michael Bayouth & Kim Klein

Nine Degrees North

Published by Palm Avenue Publishing
Printed in the United States of America

AUTHOR'S DISCLAIMER:

This novel is a work of fiction. The characters, names, incidents, dialogue, and plot are products of the author's imagination or are used fictitiously. Any resemblance to actual persons or events is purely coincidental.

~ Acknowledgements ~

Our most sincere thanks to THE FRIENDS OF KWAJ ~ we have laughed, been enlightened and reminisced right alongside you.

Special thanks to Bill Remick for sharing your expertise, John T Keeling, Sonya Haugen, Susan Remick Drout, Rod Hepburn, Mona Vento James, Vicki Vann Pack, Cindi Benn Evans, Lisa Kobayashi, Bob Barclay, Rebecca McLaughlin Sadler, Scott and Jeanette Johnson for your anecdotes and support.

Thank you also to everyone who helped us along the way, the list is long and in no way limited to the following people: Kim's parents, Joan & Kess Funk, Kim's siblings, Pamela Espinosa, Korri Brown and Michael Funk. Steve Espinosa, for your support and encouragement, Olivia Voss Klein and Bryan Brunt, for your love and unwavering belief in this project.

Thanks to Michael's dad, Ted White, who was part of the 4th Marine Division that helped take Kwajalein in World War II, to Michael's brother, Ted Bayouth, for his objectivity, Jan and Chelsea Bayouth, for reading, editing and advising us along the way, and Ben, Taylor and Beth Bayouth for their support.

Thanks to Erika Van Wingerden, Kendall Kincaid, Jim Davis, Julie and John Racoosin, Barbara Divisek, Ray Bengston, Kimberly Messadieh for your guidance and copy edit, David Matthews for your time and knowledge, Jim Hagopian for helping us with our video, and to Heather Hart—we were lost till you came along.

And finally, to the beautiful town of Carpinteria for your storybook sunsets, Starbucks for our morning lattes, The Coffee Bean and Tea Leaf for our afternoon cappuccino, Lea at the Coastal View News, Matt Roberts at the Carpinteria Department of Parks and Recreation, Heidi and Angela at Palm Lofts, Kiona Gross at the Curious Cup Book Store, Dukes of Malibu for your amazing Mai Tais, and Trader Joe's for your outrageous grapefruit juice that makes the world's best Greyhound.

This book is dedicated to
the Marshallese people

Prologue

The dawn broke dim over the vast blue ocean as a gentle tropical breeze blew inland, holding the faint sweet scent of plumeria, no doubt from a neighboring island. Although Kino was only nine years old, he was quickly becoming a fine fisherman under his grandfather's tutelage. It had taken Kino some time to master the art of throwing the heavy net.

"It is all in the gathering," his grandfather said as he looked on patiently. Kino nodded and readied himself, planting one foot on the gunwale of the outrigger and the other foot firmly on the bottom. The toss was perfect! The net landed outspread on the water just like Grandfather had taught him. Kino looked back for approval. A smile of pride transformed the old man's wrinkled face.

At that moment a blinding white flash silently engulfed everything around them, and then quickly changed, bathing the sky, the ocean, and the old man's net in crimson red.

Bravo

At critical mass, the chain reaction released the most unholy, horrendous event in the history of the United States. The 14.8-megaton explosion instantly gouged a crater 240 feet deep and over a mile wide in the island. The tops of the palm trees knelt to the sands as if they were bowing down to a mighty deity, as the explosion, a thousand times more powerful than the bomb dropped on Hiroshima, expanded. Dozens of huge, out-of-commission warships that had been placed in an array around ground zero jettisoned up the blast shaft, as gravity seemed to inverse on itself. In an instant, several million tons of radioactive debris launched skyward. Structures disintegrated. Two seconds later, the fireball was nearly three miles wide. The cloud went on to contaminate more than seven thousand square miles of the surrounding Pacific Ocean.

Seventy-Five Miles Away

On the island of Rongelap, a young group of Marshallese children were playing stickball. This was their game of choice, and Kita was winning. The sun beat down on their happy faces and life was good. But it was at that very moment, when Kita's stick smacked the ball, that everything changed forever.

A distant roar of thunder moved over the island like a giant wave. Minutes later, ashy flakes began to fall lightly from the macabre, gray sky that hung overhead. The children's game came to a halt as they stopped in wonder. The downy flakes fell silently through the tops of the tall coconut trees, landing and sticking to the beads of sweat on their young faces, filling them with a sense of awe.

Kita yelled to her mother in a nearby hut, "Mother! Come see!" Her mother emerged and stopped, speechless and confused. Off-white flakes touched down on the dark soil creating a stark contrast. The children jumped up and down, stamping out the flakes with their bare feet, creating little puffs of white powder. They began laughing and playing as the magical dust fell onto their black hair and bronzed skin. Kita's father came out of the hut and looked around, bewildered.

Little did any of them know, as the flakes continued to fall, that this could very well be the most horrific day of their lives.

SEVERAL YEARS LATER

The Marshallese people had endured the irreversible effects of radiation exposure from their tainted homeland. Marshallese men with tortured skin and withdrawn eyes crouched in the shade wherever it could be found. Undernourished children with horrific thyroid nodules and skin lesions clung to life. Stickball games were no more.

An old man carrying a bowl of water hurriedly ran through the village. He entered a hut where a pained woman was giving birth to a baby as concerned villagers looked on. Two minutes later it was born, but the baby was anything but normal. The Marshallese man's eyes widened in disbelief upon seeing the transparent, boneless, runt with stubs for limbs and a head that seemed to be joined by a second head protruding from its back. Saddened and horrified, the villagers backed slowly out of the hut.

The mother extended her arms out to the man, pleading for her newborn. The Marshallese man slowly raised the ungluing mass for her to see, but her hopeful eyes dulled as it came into view. She knew at that moment a shallow grave was being dug somewhere outside the village. It was just another in a long string of deformed births on Rongelap.

Spiral
ONE

The winter sun made no attempt to shine less brightly and remained oblivious to the happenings below. It was unapologetically beautiful in Oceanside, California, as the first shovel full of moist dirt was tossed onto the varnished oak casket, marking the end of sixteen-year-old Sara Conroy's funeral service. The year was 1967 and Sara's younger sister, Carrie, had barely turned thirteen when it happened. Carrie stared at the casket and watched in disbelief as her sister was being laid to rest, though everyone knew that the way Sara had left this world had been anything but restful.

Carrie's eyes stayed fixed on the earth as it gradually enveloped her sister, but her mind couldn't leave the event that had brought them there that day. Even though Sara had told her over and over to stay put in her parent's bedroom, she couldn't help but feel responsible for her sister's death. *If only* she had left the room, *if only* their brother Roger hadn't been away on a camping trip. Carrie couldn't stop all of the *if onlys* from playing out in her head.

Trisha, the older girl who had been present, and who was indirectly responsible for the incident occurring in the first place, stared wide-eyed into the grave. She was seventeen, a bit wild and a year older than Sara. A butterfly bandage held her bottom lip together, and she had a nasty gash on her forehead, which she had removed the band-aid from that morning so it could get some air. Her eye still showed traces of black and blue from the punch she had received during the incident. Her dark hair was blown up over her face from the buffets of chilled wind that came in off the ocean. The reality of what had happened seemed to pierce her heart like a long hatpin over and over.

It had been the year-end military ball at Camp Pendleton. The Bradfords met Carrie's parents at the Conroy house and had brought their daughter, Trisha, to hang out with the Conroy girls for the evening. Sara wasn't really fond of Trisha, but they had been thrown together because their fathers both worked at the base.

If it were up to Sara, she would just as soon have had nothing to do with her.

Carrie sat cross-legged on the king-size bed in her parents' bedroom, watching TV. It wasn't long after the girl's parents had left that Trisha had a boy over. He brought with him a brown paper bag filled with a six-pack of beer. They quickly retired to the garage, where Trisha told Sara she was going to give him a haircut. Sara knew her parents wouldn't approve, so she decided to just hang out with Carrie and watch TV.

Twenty or so minutes later, Sara heard the sound of water running and went to investigate. When she returned to the bedroom, Carrie could see that she was very upset. Trisha and the boy were apparently taking a shower together in the bathroom and had locked the door. Sara sternly told Carrie to stay put and went back out into the hall. She placed her ear up against the bathroom door and could hear the two of them talking. Trisha's muffled voice asked, *What was that pill you gave me, I feel so light-headed.*

The boy replied, *Just go with it. Man, you have an amazing body.*

Sara shook her head, fuming, when suddenly she heard Trisha scream, *"STOP IT!"* The sound of a *slap* rang out, which was followed by the sound of a solid punch and a body hitting the floor. Sara was frightened and shouted through the door, "That's it. I'm calling the cops right now!"

From the bedroom Carrie could hear the commotion. She got up and turned the volume down on the TV, pacing back and forth, not knowing what to do. Should she go out there? Sara had been firm when she told her to stay put, and Carrie was scared. As much as she wanted to investigate and see what was happening, fear overtook her instead and she went back and sat on the bed, keeping perfectly still, as she stared at the muted television screen. At least twenty minutes passed and the house had become deadly silent when she got the nerve to leave the room. She found Trisha out cold, bleeding on the bathroom floor. Carrie raced around the house, frantically looking for her sister. She saw the phone receiver hanging from its coiled cord from the wall phone in the kitchen. At that moment two policemen entered through the open front door. One of the policemen found Sara out back but prevented Carrie from going out there. He escorted her out to the police car where they stayed until the ambulance came. This ultimately would be the worst night of Carrie's life.

~~~~~~~

When the funeral was over, Carrie's mother, Joanna, approached Trisha. Joanna's red nose poked out from underneath her dark sunglasses that covered her eyes, which were blood red from days on end of crying. Calm and quiet, Joanna spoke through a huge lump in her throat.

"Trisha, I just want you to know that Sara was my first baby—my very first." Joanna dabbed a tissue at the bottom of her sunglasses.

"I don't suppose you will know how special that is until you're a mother. When she was two she used to pull flowers out from my prize-winning flower garden and give them to me. She'd say, *Mommy, these are for you.* The momentary smile brought by the memory quickly faded from Joanna's face and was replaced by one of pure disdain.

"I will *never* forgive you for letting that boy into our house, and for what he did to my daughter, do you hear me? *NEV-ER!*"

Major Conroy, who was standing with several officers from the military, did a double-take when he saw Joanna talking to Trisha and ran over to get her. Trisha held her hands to her face and felt the world caving in on her. As Major Conroy led Joanna off, she kept her head craned around, looking at Trisha. Sadly, it was no more than two days later that Trisha was found dead, having taken her own life with pain pills from her mother's medicine cabinet. With no one left to testify, the boy was never caught. Both of these facts just added salt to the already unfathomable wound endured by the Conroy family.

~~~~~~

Two years later, Carrie Conroy was now fifteen years old. It had been a rough transition adjusting to life without Sara. Shortly after Sara's death, Carrie's parents presented her with a horse. He was a beautiful black Arabian that she named Geronimo, "Moe" for short, and he quickly became her whole world.

Her older brother, Roger, was sixteen. His signature brown, unkempt, curly hair and sinewy build, along with his lackadaisical gait, gave Roger a definitive style all his own. On the outside, he seemed to be more resilient to the upheaval that had befallen their family, though he carried a quiet resentment towards the reality of the situation. He immersed himself in football as much as possible, watching it and playing it. Roger didn't like to talk about Sara, it hurt too much. At dinners he'd excuse himself from the table if conversations shifted to her. The loss was real for all of them, but Roger's pain was somehow different. All the talking and good memories didn't make Roger feel better. His mourning was private. Whatever scar it had left on him was deep inside and he did not want to share it with anyone.

Carrie arrived home after school and tramped up the rear steps to the back door, carrying her books. She walked in and froze for a moment at the sight of the kitchen in disarray. Her mother, Joanna, was baking. It was something she rarely did, unless there was some new power wife on the Rotary she wanted to impress, or, in this case, a simple attempt to replicate some form of normality.

Carrie's after-school routine usually consisted of setting her books down on the counter and grabbing a cold Fresca out of the icebox. But today, flour, batter bowls, buttered cookie sheets, and cookbooks covered every inch of counter space. Exasperated, Carrie blew the bangs out of her face. "Mom, you destroyed the kitchen."

Joanna glanced back over her shoulder and said, "Oh, hi, honey. Yeah, I know, sorry. I've never made these before. It's taken a few batches to get them right. How was school?" Before Carrie could answer, Joanna continued, "Oh, sweetheart, I have a few things I need to talk to you about."

"What's that?" Carried asked, still holding her schoolbooks.

The timer went off and Joanna's attention was called back to the oven. She slipped potholders over her hands, turned and said, "Well, remember I mentioned to you that General Mitchell and his family transferred from here to Kwajalein last year, that island in the Pacific? Well, your father put in for the same transfer a few months back, and guess what? He got it. We'll be moving there, too. It'll give us a chance at a fresh start, and you and Roger will love—"

"What about Geronimo?" Carrie asked firmly, cutting her off.

"Well, that's one of the things that I need to talk to you about," Joanna said as she carefully pulled a fresh batch of teacakes out of the oven. "He'll stay at Overlook Farms until—"

At that moment a loud *bang* almost caused Joanna to drop the cookie sheet she was holding. It sounded like a gun had discharged in her kitchen. Joanna spun around to find Carrie gone. The back door was wide open, her books were on the floor, and the kitchen rug was scrunched up like an accordion. Joanna set down the sheet of teacakes, walked to the back door, and looked out to see Carrie sprinting up the hill toward Overlook Farms, the horse stables at the end of the road where Moe was boarded.

The thought of losing Moe left Carrie emotionally shattered. She couldn't stand the mere thought of it. They had been together now for two years, and each day that they spent together their bond became that much stronger. He was her solid. When she was on his back the pain inside her from missing Sara didn't hurt as much, they became one, she couldn't differentiate between the two of them.

She sobbed uncontrollably as she saddled Moe, slipped his riding bridle on him, hopped onto his back, and took off. At a full gallop, Carrie stroked Moe's neck with one hand while holding the reins tight with the other. Trails of windblown tears moved back over her temples and were absorbed into her hair. Her entire world was cracking in two, and she could feel the crushing pain of loss returning again.

She stopped Moe at the top of the hill overlooking the ocean. It was a fair day and San Clemente Island was clearly visible. She couldn't imagine living somewhere like that, completely surrounded by water. She dismounted from Moe and led him under the shade of a large oak tree.

"Hey, big guy," she said softly to the gentle giant. Moe twisted his strong neck to face her. Carrie touched his muzzle and he playfully nudged her back. She stroked and scratched the long white blaze on his face and leaned her forehead against his, feeling the hot breath from his flared nostrils.

"You know I love you, right, Moe?"

He seemed to be listening carefully, his dark brown eyes softly focused. Carrie clenched her teeth and shook her head, knowing the inevitable.

"God dammit!" Then holding both sides of his bridal and looking him straight in the eyes she said, "I have to leave for a while, Moe. But I'm not leaving you, understand? And don't think for a minute that this is my choice. It's not." Carrie rubbed her face against his as Moe let out a slight whinny. This was killing her. The hole inside Carrie ripped open a little wider. The spiral of Sara, and now Moe, spinning away from her was almost too much to bear.

Carrie and Moe stayed there on that hill overlooking the island in thought until the sun, like Carrie's heavy heart, sank below the horizon. It was now dusk and she slowly walked Moe back to the stables, while singing Sara's favorite Joni Mitchell song, *The Circle Game*. She didn't want to go back home, she was already home. And it was right here, with Moe.

Kwajalein
TWO

A fter talking with her family about the move over dinner that night, and looking at a map, all Carrie really knew was that Kwajalein was a very small island, about three miles long by a half-mile wide. It was nine hundred miles north of the equator in the Marshall Atoll and was surrounded by what looked like a zillion miles of endless ocean, just a little dot somewhere in the middle of the Pacific. Her father, Major Conroy, tried painting a rosy picture of sandy tropical beaches, beautiful and exotic, but all that mattered to her was that it was almost five thousand miles away from Overlook Farms, where her heart was boarded.

As Carrie's world was being obliterated once again, she knew she didn't have a say in the matter. Her mother had assured her that Moe would be taken care of by her trainer while they were gone, and that he would be hers again when they returned to the mainland after her father's tour was over. This made it a little less painful, but just barely so. Her heart ached in a way she hadn't experienced since she'd lost Sara. A sickness settled in her stomach that wouldn't go away.

There was little time to live with the news before the actual move and that was probably a good thing. Carrie didn't have much time to mourn, or to engage in long good-byes. It seemed like before the news really sank in and became a reality, the moving van was already parked out front, taking away their things, their home, their life, and storing them all somewhere unseen. Carrie and Roger were left with only their brand spankin' new Samsonite suitcases in hand, and a one-way ticket to Kwajalein.

Departure
THREE

The first leg of the trip to Kwajalein was aboard a commercial airliner, a United 747 to Honolulu. The plane wasn't full, and once in the air they were told they were free to move around and could even sit in different seats if they liked. Carrie found an entire row for herself, and with her legs outstretched and ankles crossed read a *Teen* magazine and sipped pineapple juice garnished with a tiny Asian-print umbrella. Everything about the flight so far indicated that she was already in a tropical paradise.

She found herself watching the stewardesses as they went from row to row, taking drink orders, bringing pillows, and turning off little call lights. One of them reminded Carrie of Sara, with the same long, dark, flowing hair and deep-set brown eyes. She still couldn't believe Sara was gone and was never coming back.

She looked down at the charm bracelet on her wrist that Sara had given to her on her thirteenth birthday. Sara had picked it out herself and had bought three very special charms for her to start off her collection. There was a sand dollar, the kind of shell that the two of them always searched for on their yearly family vacations up in Carpinteria, her own name *Carrie* and one that simply said *Sisters*. Carrie lovingly touched each charm. It was the one thing she had that always made her feel connected to Sara and she very seldom ever took it off. Sara had told her that it was her *good luck charm* and that she should always wear it because there was no such thing as a girl having too much luck.

Once they landed in Honolulu, an abrupt and disappointing change awaited her. The next leg of the flight to Kwajalein would be on a C-130 military transport plane. There were no stewardesses, no in-flight meals or snacks, and definitely no pineapple juice. Carrie felt a shift in her optimistic mood as all the tropical colors faded to drab green and military gray.

She couldn't get comfortable in the rear-facing seat of the plane. The roar of the engines was almost deafening, and it hurt her ears. She covered them periodically in frustration with the palms of her hands between turning the pages of her *Teen* magazine. There were no windows, and when she looked up at the ceiling, squinting, something wet would drip down on her. It felt like oil or some other slick substance that had a slightly unpleasant odor. After many swipes with a tissue to her forehead, she finally reached into her carry-on and retrieved the small umbrella that her mother had insisted she pack in case of a tropical storm. She clicked off the umbrella's safety latch, raised it open, and begrudgingly held it over her head.

This annoyed Roger, who was sitting next to her. "What are you doing? Put that thing away!" he snapped as he elbowed her.

"No! Something gross is dripping on me."

Just then, a tall, young man in military fatigues walked down the aisle, glanced at her umbrella, and snickered. From the corner of his mouth he said, "The weather forecast for the rest of the flight is warm and dry, with only a slight chance of rain."

He handed her a can of Fresca and tossed Roger a Coke. Carrie peered up from under the umbrella and caught sight of his nametag: Lieutenant Ryan Mitchell.

Ryan Mitchell was the young son of General Mitchell. General Mitchell was the highest-ranking officer on the island, the man in charge, which on the little island of Kwajalein was the equivalent to royalty.

"Thanks," she said glumly as she took the soda from his hand and looked up at his face. His steely blue eyes were intense, and Carrie couldn't look at him for long without having to turn away. It was like looking at the sun, stinging and burning. She couldn't quite pinpoint it, but there was something about him that made her feel uneasy.

"Cheer up, kid. It may not be Club Med, but you're gonna like it, trust me," he said, turning to leave.

Major Conroy observed the interaction between Carrie and the military man and was somewhat embarrassed by his daughter's odd umbrella-holding behavior. Major Conroy had just packed his pipe and begun to light it when he called to the lieutenant, "Excuse me, can I get a scotch rocks over here?"

Ryan Mitchell turned sharply and retorted, "I'm not a waiter, sir. I'm Lieutenant Ryan Mitchell, General Mitchell's son."

Major Conroy saluted him. "Ahh, yes. Pardon me, I saw you with the sodas and made an assumption. I'm Major Conroy, I've worked with your father for many years."

Ryan Mitchell saluted back.

"Welcome to Kwajalein Missile Range, Major. Hope you and your family will enjoy living on the island."

Ryan gave Carrie a once-over and then looked to Major Conroy.

"It's going to be quite an adjustment. Not like living on the mainland."

Major Conroy took a deep draw from his pipe. "Yes, well, we'll adapt," he replied, pursing his lips.

Ryan saluted the Major again, turned sharply on his heels, and walked back to the front of the plane.

There was something about Ryan, as if he were trying too hard. Even though he wore two rows of ribbon bars that commanded an air of respect, you knew he probably would never earn them. His good looks and tall, lean body made the hours he spent working out quite obvious and gave him the appearance of a Ken doll or GI Joe. Ryan kept himself meticulously well groomed, trimmed his light brown crew cut every two weeks, and plucked the few straggling eyebrows that framed his blue eyes. He always smelled faintly of Hai Karate aftershave, and his friends joked that he bought the stuff only because it came with an instruction manual on how to fight off all of the women that this "manly" scent was guaranteed to attract. Ryan didn't find the accusation amusing in the least, and, of course, he denied it.

Ryan worked hard every day to maintain the military academy image that had been expected of him and drilled into his head since he was born. He wanted nothing more than to shine in the eyes of his father, which he found to be a constant challenge. He was forever taunted by his father's words, *Be a real man*, which he had heard since he was a young boy, like a scratchy 45, that played over and over in his head.

Kwaj Podge
FOUR

Nestor Benga showed up early Saturday morning in a rusted old golf cart. As the director of the Teen Center, a large part of his job on the island was to welcome the young new residents. Nestor had lived on Kwaj for the past seven years, arriving at the age of eighteen to accept his first job as a baggage handler at the Kwajalein airport. After putting in a couple of years there, he had heard that the Teen Center was looking for a new director and he jumped at the opportunity. Coming from a large Samoan family of eleven children, he had helped his mother care for, protect, and be responsible for his many siblings. He had a calm and gentle demeanor, and though he was a man of few words, the ones that he chose to speak always seemed full of wisdom.

The first thing on his agenda was to give Roger and Carrie a tour around the island. Carrie heard the hum of the little cart pulling up in front of the house before she actually saw it. She came bounding out, while Roger shuffled slowly behind her.

"Good morning." Nestor smiled and squinted beneath his dark sunglasses.

"Noddah bootiful morning here in paradise, no?" Nestor asked in his pidgin English.

"Yeah, it sure is." Carrie exclaimed as she jumped in the back seat.

Roger took a seat in the front, wiping the sweat off his brow from the already baking day.

"Where we off to, Nestor?"

"Ah, you lucky. You get local tour… actually, everyone local here before too long. Kwaj no tourist destination."

As the little golf cart bumpily headed off down the street and away from the house, the blue skies, warm trade winds, and coconut-packed palms could have fooled anyone into thinking that they were, indeed, at one of the world's most desirable vacation destinations.

Nestor glanced over at Roger and noticed his head was down and his arms were crossed. "Roger, you sleeping behind those Foster Grants?"

Roger immediately straightened up and brushed his shaggy brown hair away from his face.

"No, no, I'm awake."

Nestor rounded the corner and pointed to a nondescript building.

"There lot to do here on island. Over there is Teen Center. Most popular place for kids. Of course, that where I work—probably reason so popular." He gave a big smile.

Carrie smiled too.

"What do they do there, Nestor?"

Nestor said, "Oh, let's see, many thing. Play pool, pinball, have dance, listen to music. Just fun place hang out." Nestor took off his glasses with one hand and wiped the condensation off with the bottom of his black HANG LOOSE T-shirt before putting them back on.

"There is also movie on weekend at Richardson Theater. We have snack bar—that fun place to meet friends. And they serve best fried rice and pepper steak. Of course, always beach. Water ski, swim, fish. Best beach in world."

They drove farther along Lagoon Road, which seemed to be shared with only an occasional military vehicle or a passing bicycle. Roger could feel the hot sun already leaving a burn on his exposed arm, and he moved a little closer to the middle of the cart, hoping Nestor wouldn't notice.

Roger leaned in and asked, "Do they have sharks here?"

Nestor nodded his head.

"Oh, yes, many." Pointing off in the direction they were headed, he said, "They feed shark every day at shark pit near missile base so they no hungry—keep them away from swimming area. Always best be careful, though."

"Wow, what's that?" Roger said, pointing to a huge, round, white structure by the runway.

Nestor replied, "What, that thing? That radar ball for military use."

Roger continued with his questioning.

"What does the military do way out here in the middle of the Pacific Ocean, anyway? Our dad doesn't really tell us that much."

Nestor smiled and said matter-of-factly, "They test nuclear rocket." Raising his hands and wiggling his fingers, he added, "All very top secret."

They drove for a while in silence. He showed them the Richardson Movie Theater, Surfway Market, and the 10-10 convenience store. The kids had to laugh, being familiar with Safeway and 7-11 in the States.

Nestor pointed to a metal building.

"See building over there? That photo lab. They have darkroom for you to learn develop your own film. Sometimes kids use darkroom for hanky-panky, too."

Roger smiled.

"My dad just bought me a really cool Nikon before we left the States. This place might not be so bad after all."

"Yes, good place to be," Nestor said. "Kids here have lots freedom. Oh, and in evening every night, air-raid siren go off. Don't let scare you—most people use as dinner bell."

Just then a small pickup with a caged shell on the back drove by them with an official-looking emblem on the side door. Roger followed the truck with his eyes as it passed.

"Is that a dogcatcher or something?"

"No, that policeman, Curtis. Only policeman on island." Nestor leaned in, "Not very smart. He only catch kids drinking at golf course. They put beer vending machine at fourth hole for adult. Hard keep kids away though." Roger and Carrie both laughed.

Carrie pointed to a huge derelict ship that was upside-down by the shore.

"What's that?" she asked.

"*Prinz Eugen,*" Nestor replied.

"Nazi warship that was blown up with other ships at Bikini Island, *BIG* nuclear bomb test."

"Here?" asked Roger.

To that Nestor answered, "Well, not here, but not far from here."

Roger and Carrie exchanged a look of concern.

The Acclimation

FIVE

It took a month or so for Carrie and Roger to adjust to island life. Carrie's thoughts of Sara and Moe were less frequent now that she had made new friends, although the pictures she kept of them both on her dresser still drew upon her a deep longing that Carrie just couldn't shake—and, for that matter, didn't want to.

Roger had snagged a football magazine from the Teen Center and plastered the walls in his bedroom with football photos of his favorite team, the Dallas Cowboys. The absence of TV on the island made following games completely futile, so this was going to have to suffice in the interim. Besides, he had his new Nikon to fill his time with. Experimenting with two

31

lenses, f-stops, shutter speeds, and mastering depth of field was more than enough to keep his brain occupied, instead of thinking about point spreads and who was headed for the Super Bowl.

There were certain things that took a little more time getting adjusted to, like showering several times a day due to the extreme humidity. And it also took a little time to make peace with the small white geckos that seemed to Velcro themselves to the interior white walls of their cinder block house every night. This would cause Carrie to let out a slight gasp when she entered the bathroom and saw them, evenly spaced out like *Art Gecko* wallpaper, as she liked to put it. She would move very slowly to keep them from scurrying about, because that was when she got nervous. She was fine if they would just stay still.

At times, when Carrie got homesick, she would go sit on the pier in the evening and stare out at the ocean, believing that she could see California in the distance, when in reality all she could see was the silhouette of a neighboring island. She found it comforting knowing that her old world still existed, even if for now she could only see it in her mind's eye. But for the most part, things were better here than she ever could have imagined. Nestor was right, just as he had told them, there was a lot to do and they were given an incredible amount of freedom. Every day seemed to hold the promise of a new adventure.

When the tropical rains came to the island, they weren't like any of the rainstorms Carrie had ever witnessed in California. These were quick, hot, and delightful. No sooner had they arrived than they would quickly disappear, leaving a sunny day behind them.

It was Saturday morning, and Carrie and her new friends Gina, Tess, and Donna were riding their bikes over to the Teen Center when a tropical storm came through.

The girls had all become best friends since they first arrived on the island. Gina was sixteen, full of confidence and more than likely the leading lady in many island boys' wet dreams, at least until Farrah Fawcett came along. Blonde and leggy, she was aware of her undeniable sex appeal and wielded it without discrimination. She always seemed able to go with the flow and never got caught up in the serious stuff; she was the epitome of cool.

Then there was Tess, who was a bit rough around the edges but had a heart of gold. Tess was a tomboy. With no discernible waist and narrow hips, she barely stood five feet tall, and that was when she was practicing her best posture. She was witty, with a deep card catalog and a quick retrieval system. At times, an underlying sadness rose to her surface, hinting at possible hurts and unresolved issues that lived within the tough-guy walls that she had built around her.

Tess's older sister, Donna, was genuinely sweet and a natural beauty. With her bedroom eyes and long dark hair, she had been compared several times to a young Liz Taylor. She was a hopeless romantic whose weakness was falling for guys at the drop of a hat. Even though Donna's beauty and to-die-for bust line made Carrie feel inadequate and invisible at times, Carrie also hoped that possibly, just by being in her presence, some of those physical attributes might conceivably rub off on her.

Pedaling their bikes at full speed, they tried to outrun the rain. It was a game they liked to play, though they never won, and today was no exception. Laughing, the rain-soaked girls rode toward the Teen Center as they passed the missile control facility.

Inside the facility, in front of a bank of monitors, sat a row of control room operators. One of the operators spoke into his microphone.

"Skies are clear now, sir. Winds are southeast at eleven point five miles per hour." He listened momentarily for a reply and then continued, "We're a go for liftoff. Initiating countdown sequence."

Another operator moved in to his microphone.

"Ten, nine, eight, seven, six, five, four, three, two, one, ignition."

As the girls pulled up to the Teen Center and parked their bikes in the rack outside, a loud rumbling startled them, it seemed as if they were about to experience an earthquake. A bright explosion of orange light lit up the sky as the smoke and fire of a rocket lifting off illuminated the nearby missile test facility. This was the first time since their arrival on Kwaj that they had actually witnessed a missile launch, and they stood watching as the rocket quickly pulled away from its platform with a trembling thunder. Roger came running out of the center with his camera in hand, turned, and quickly ran back inside to retrieve his long lens. In seconds he was back outside. He attached the lens and, with head up, quickly began taking photographs of the ascending rocket.

Still soaked from the quickly passing storm, the dripping girls brushed by Roger and ran inside, shaking their heads like a bunch of wet dogs. The Teen Center had a few pool tables and magazines and played music most of the time. Nestor was behind the counter, reading a local island rag, while a couple of the girls' guy friends, Adam and Billy, were hanging out.

Adam looked up from shooting pool and said, "Well, well, well, look what the cat dragged in."

Adam was sixteen and seemingly oblivious of his good looks and great physique. The girls all loved him. He was the type that could do a pull-up with one hand while rolling a joint with the other. And if his good looks and physical talents were not enough, he could charm them with his smile and his occasional propensity for reciting Shakespeare.

Donna wiped her eyes and noticed the smears of mascara on her fingers, "God, why do I even bother putting on make-up?"

Tess huffed and replied, "Because you're a girly girl. Might as well get used to it Donna, we're not in Kansas anymore."

Nestor leaned over the counter and tossed the girls a few towels. They began to dry off vigorously. Gina bent over, tossing her hair forward and wrapped it up in the towel.

"Well, I love it here. The rain doesn't bother me. I adapt. I'm a chameleon."

Adam jumped at this, "Wonder what color you'd turn if you crawled on me?"

A Cheshire cat smile spread across Adam's tan face, which was immediately nailed by Gina's wet towel.

Tess glanced over at Donna's nipplage on her considerably larger breasts and pulled her own wet shirt away from her skin.

"Wow, looks like I lost the wet T-shirt contest." Gina laughed out loud.

"I'd say you all won," said Billy from the corner. Carrie rolled her eyes.

Billy was playing the Cosmos pinball machine. He was sixteen, lanky, and a dead ringer for John Lennon. He looked up for a moment and then went back to his game. He had accumulated the high score of 66,000,000 points after many hours of time and effort, making him the new top dog.

"Yessss!" he said excitedly, as he tore himself away from the game and approached the girls.

"Can anybody really lose a wet T-shirt contest? Huh, Adam?"

Tess scrunched up her face.

"Ewww, shut up, Billy."

Carrie looked down at her own wet shirt stuck to her smaller breasts and modestly covered herself with crossed arms.

"This is so embarrassing. I'm never going anywhere again without wearing my bathing suit under my clothes."

Gina looked over at Carrie. With her hands on her hips, she proudly exclaimed, "What's your problem? It's not a big deal, Carrie. It's called the human body."

Adam, still admiring the view, said, "To quote my friend Billiam, *What's in a name? That which we call a rose by any other name would smell as sweet.*"

Gina, making no attempt to conceal her breasts, couldn't help but smile.

~~~~~~~

Back at the missile control center, one of the operators spoke into his mic.

"Winds subsided to four point two miles per hour, sir."

Another control room operator snapped to attention and quickly eyeballed his monitor. His face revealed a tense concern. He slid over to a mic and switched it on.

"Attention: Light wind scenario warning. All personnel, light wind scenario warning."

Several military personnel grabbed binoculars and moved to the window. Another operator began flipping switches frantically as he swung into emergency protocol mode.

Inside the Teen Center, Billy joined Adam at the pool table.

"I gotta write my brother Ted and tell 'im I just beat his ass at Cosmos. He's held the top score at UC Berkeley forever."

Billy's brother Ted was twenty-two, a student and political activist. Billy looked up to Ted a great deal and wanted nothing more than to emulate him and make him proud. Ted had turned him on to the peace movement, the New Left, and underground literature like the *Berkeley Tribe*. Billy absorbed all that was Ted, it made him feel like they were still part of one another's life, that a measly 4,750 miles was no more of a distance between them than their old bedrooms at the opposite ends of the house.

"That'll piss 'im off," Adam scoffed.

"Hey, Gina, by the way, me and Billy were thinking of going fishing over at the shark pit by the base tomorrow. You girls wanna come?"

Nestor, overhearing this, looked up and chimed in, "How 'bout I teach you all to climb coconut tree instead? More fun, and if fall, you don't get eaten by shark. Shark pit not safest place to be on island."

Outside the Teen Center, Roger excitedly snapped off pictures of the rocket and the billowing cloud trail, which just seemed to hang there against the blue sky, not moving at all. The booster stage separated as the rocket continued up through the stratosphere. Roger smiled, knowing this would make for some spectacular photographs. Then he realized something was not quite right. He stopped and slowly pulled the camera away from his face as he paled at his realization. The booster stage looked as if it was coming directly back down, very close to the trail of clouds the rocket had left on its ascent. Which could only mean one thing: it was heading directly back to the island! At first he shook his head in disbelief as he thought, *Can this really be happening?* Personnel from the military base begin to stream outside with binoculars, which confirmed Roger's suspicions.

Roger yelled at the top of his lungs, "Holy shit! Incoming nuke!"

Nestor and the kids ran outside to see what the commotion was about. Roger pointed up as he took off running.

"Run, you guys! *Run!*"

Carrie looked up and staggered backward, blinded by the glare of the sky and backed into the wall of the Teen Center behind her. She shielded her eyes but saw nothing, then suddenly stood motionless. The booster stage was now visible and was heading directly at them. Donna saw Carrie making no attempt to move and screamed at her.

"For Christ's sake, *Carrie, run!*"

Donna and the others took off. Watching the rocket descend, Carrie slid down the side of the wall and curled up into a fetal position with her arms over her head. Nestor, who was oblivious to Carrie, ran back into the Teen Center and dove behind the counter.

The island siren began to sound the emergency. A half-mile away Joanna looked up from doing the dishes. Several fishermen with their gear down at the marina turned to look. One of them pointed at the rapidly descending booster stage. *"What the... Look!"*

Back at the Teen Center, the kids scattered in all directions. A shadow grew over the building as if it were about to be swallowed up. Roger glanced back over his shoulder and saw the rocket booster narrowly miss the Teen Center as it embedded itself into the ground. The massive explosion from the impact blew out the glass windows of the center and sent the teens hurtling off their feet. The immense collision reverberated throughout the island, as a giant red cloud instantly formed, plunging a several-acre radius into an unearthly rust-colored shadow. A large mushroom ring of dust quickly billowed up into the sky.

Carrie's seemingly lifeless body fell over, covered in a layer of dust, leaving a clean, white silhouette of her body's outline on the wall. Nestor grabbed a towel off the floor and put it over his mouth. He came barreling out into the dust cloud amid the broken glass and debris, looked around, and saw Carrie. Rushing over to her, he said, "Carrie! You okay? *Carrie!*"

She coughed as Nestor wiped the dirt and dust away from her mouth. He noticed a small shard of glass protruding from her ankle and carefully removed it. She slowly opened her eyes and smiled up at him. He cocked his head and said, "Actually, shark pit maybe not so dangerous after all."

Carrie laughed, and Nestor smiled with relief, knowing she was okay. She sat up, and he helped her to her feet.

Not far away, Roger got up, brushed himself off, and checked his camera to see if it had been damaged. He rushed over to the rocket and began taking more pictures. From out of nowhere several military personnel arrived all at once. An MP saw Roger taking pictures and immediately confiscated his Nikon, saying, "Security kid. No cameras."

Roger gave him a dirty look. The MP stared gravely at Roger before walking away with Roger's new Nikon. The large rocket smoked, and appeared to be embedded into the ground a good fifteen to twenty feet. The earth all around was cracked and smoldering. From the look on the faces of the kids, now safe and regrouped, it was obvious they had a newfound respect for this unpredictable and treacherous place they now called home.

The Conroys

SIX

After having cleaned up at the Teen Center, Roger and Carrie came rushing through the front door, their energy level still high from all the excitement of the afternoon. Roger raced straight to his room and dropped his empty camera bag on his bed, while Carrie went into the kitchen.

Maru, the Marshallese maid, was busy setting the table and barely looked up. Her limited English had left her feeling insecure, and, as a result, quiet and soft-spoken. She was a young woman in her mid-twenties. Like many of the Marshallese, her thick skin was the color of French roast coffee with just a splash of cream. She had kinky jet-black hair and wide-set eyes. Her contagious smile was wide as well, with teeth that were stained yellow from too much coffee, cigarettes, and lack of dental hygiene.

Carrie walked past Maru to her mother, who was in the kitchen, nervously pacing between stove and sink. "Hi, Mom."

Joanna dropped a spatula and turned to Carrie.

"Oh, my God, you're okay! I'm so glad you're safe! I heard the siren, and your father just told me that a rocket crashed somewhere near the Teen Center."

Carrie grabbed a Fresca out of the icebox.

"Oh, Mom, you don't need to worry. Besides, it was nowhere near us."

Roger entered the kitchen and swiped the hair back off his forehead.

"Hey, Mom, dig this. You should've seen it. It was unbelievable. The rocket fell right in front of us. I got pictures of the whole thing, but they took my damn camera."

Carrie shot a look at Roger, as Joanna shot a look at Carrie.

"Oh, *really?* Nowhere near it?" Joanna said, holding up her hands, "You're both alive—that's all that matters."

Quickly changing the subject, Joanna glanced at the clock, "Look, Maru can't miss her six o'clock boat back to Ebeye, and we still have a few things left to do. One of you go feed Magoo and Snoop."

Roger looked at his sister.

"I just fed 'em last night. Your turn, *Canary.*"

Carrie glared at Roger.

"Don't call me that, *Rover!*"

Mr. Magoo, the tabby cat that they had inherited with the house, rubbed against Carrie's legs and wound himself around her ankles as she grabbed the bag of Cat Chow from under the counter and filled his bowl. Snoop waited patiently nearby for Carrie to turn her attention to him. Snoop was a lovable little mixed-breed dog that had also come with the house when they moved in. They guessed he was around five years old. He was tricolored, a long hot-dog type with short legs and a head that was much too big for his body.

Joanna was relieved that her children were safe and went back to cooking dinner. She could be heard throughout the house as she hummed *Que Sera, Sera* by Doris Day, which was one of her favorites, as well as one that Carrie and Roger loved to hear, as it meant that their mother was content. Carrie also hoped that this time it meant that her mother had already forgotten about the little white lie Carrie had tried to slip by her.

Dinner was served promptly at five thirty, as Major Conroy not only preferred this, but also expected it. Carrie and Roger took their designated places at the table, and Joanna began to pass the platter of fried chicken. Dinnertime had not been the same since Sara had died. There was always a reminder that something, or in this case, that *someone*, was missing. Before, everyone had shared their stories of the day, and there was laughter and a feeling of unity at the dinner table.

Now, it always seemed to take on a more somber tone, knowing that they were all feeling the same emptiness that even a wonderful meal couldn't fill.

Maru was in the living room, packing up her purse. She grabbed her scarf and walked by the dinner table on her way out the back door.

"Good night, Conroys. See you tomorrow."

Joanna and Carrie thanked Maru and wished her a good night, while Roger talked intently with his father about the happenings of the day.

"What about my camera, Dad? They can't just take my camera, can they?"

Major Conroy picked through the platter and selected a thigh and a leg, fried to a perfect golden brown.

"Don't worry, Rog, you'll get it back. They just want the film. You'll probably get it back in a day or two."

Roger took a big bite of creamed corn and said with a full mouth, "I don't know what the big deal is. It's just a rocket stuck in the dirt."

Major Conroy held up his glass of milk and cringed.

"I don't think I'm ever going to get used to this damn powdered milk."

Joanna smiled at her husband and placed her hand on his shoulder, giving it a light squeeze.

"Well, it's better than having water with your cereal in the morning, isn't it?"

Major Conroy's claim to living-room fame was his impersonation of Henry Kissinger.

"Dat's debatable," he said, in his best Henry.

Roger cracked up. It was the first time his father had joked at the dinner table in years. He always loved it when his dad climbed down from his military flagpole. Both Roger and Carrie severely missed seeing this lighter side of him.

"Dad, give us some more of your Kissinger. You do him *so* good!"

Major Conroy looked over the top of his glass at his son.

"Nope, that's it. I only bring Henry out at parties."

"Come on, Dad," Roger urged. Everyone at the table was quiet.

Then, unexpectedly and in his deep monotone voice, Major Conroy said, "Vot is dat, a steak he's e-teen?"

Everyone laughed, including Major Conroy himself. Carrie and Roger exchanged a hopeful glance at each other. Hearing their father joke, as well as seeing the physical touch between their parents, seemed a huge milestone since the family had lost Sara. There were times in the past few years when both Roger and Carrie thought that divorce was inevitable and maybe, just maybe, these little exchanges were a sign that the family was healing.

Quickly composing himself, their father said, "So, kids, on a serious note, your mother and I are leaving in a few days for a short vacation to Hawaii. You guys will be in charge here, and I trust you will handle yourselves responsibly. We'll be back on the sixteenth."

Carrie and Roger shot each other an excited glance, which didn't escape Major Conroy.

"I saw that look." He stared Carrie in the eye and then landed on Roger. "Don't be thinking you'll be having any parties here." He used his index finger like a jackhammer on the dinner table.

"And there will be *no* boating, *no* waterskiing, and absolutely *no* visiting the fourth hole, which I'm sure you didn't think we knew about."

Carrie objected, "Ahh, Dad!"

Roger set his glass down on the table.

"So, in other words, we can't have any fun at all?"

Major Conroy did not feel like arguing, nor did he see any need for compromise. His looked sternly at his son.

"No, Roger, in those *very* words. Now, this conversation's over."

Exiled

SEVEN

It was nearing six o'clock, and the *Tarlang* was about to leave Kwaj. A long line of Marshallese workers waited to board her, as this ferryboat was their only transportation between work and home. Maru took her place in line as she pulled off her scarf, let her hair down, and lit a cigarette. There was a pit in her stomach which seemed to arrive like clockwork, every night, at just about the same time the *Tarlang* pulled up to the dock.

As the military missile-testing program grew on Kwajalein in the 1950s, the United States had relocated the Marshallese residents to a small planned community on the nearby island of Ebeye. The Marshallese commuted from Ebeye to Kwajalein each day, where they worked in a variety of jobs, including domestic help for many American families. They were made to return to the island of Ebeye each night.

At that time, Carrie and her friends weren't aware that the Marshallese were only allowed on Kwajalein during working hours. They never really even thought much about it. Here they were, living as uninvited guests on this island, and the Marshallese themselves weren't even allowed to live there, not even to stay past six o'clock. They had no idea that when Maru and the other Marshallese left each evening, they weren't really going home, sadly, they were leaving it.

Keep Your Eye on the Coconut
EIGHT

The radioactive remains of a death-dealing machine protruded from the lagoon and were part of the view as they knew it. The pillage of these lagoon shipwrecks became a regular pastime for the kids on Kwaj, even though the *Prinz Eugen* was a Nazi warship and, in a sense, it was both a memorial to the dual horrors it represented and a reminder of those two dark chapters in human history.

The *Prinz Eugen* was confiscated after World War II and then nuked with other target ships at Bikini Island. After surviving the Bikini nuclear tests, the *Prinz Eugen* was towed to Kwaj, where it was moored at the pier for some time. Eventually the mooring ropes got old and broke loose during a storm, and the wreck drifted and overturned by the shore, where it found its final resting place.

Roger, Adam, and Billy sat atop its house-sized, rusted propeller, which protruded from the water by the beach. As they spray-painted their names on it, Nestor approached them from the shore.

"I wonder if it's still radioactive," he said. "Amazing to think that it rubbed elbows with one of the largest nuclear tests of all time."

This got their attention.

"What?" Billy asked.

"Oh, nevah mind," Nestor replied calmly, as he headed for the shade of a large coconut tree on the beach. Barely a moment had passed before the three boys were by his side, vigorously wiping the rust from their bathing suits and their bodies.

Later Carrie, Tess, and Gina joined the group, and Nestor began the lesson he had promised them on climbing coconut trees. Nestor squinted and looked up toward the top of the tree.

"Da secret is, pick one coconut and keep your eye on it. Grip da tree tightly with your arms, hold most of your weight on feet, and basically hop up da tree."

Demonstrating, Nestor made it look easy, reaching the top and making his way back down again.

"Piece a cake," said Adam, pulling off his shirt to reveal his toned physique. The others glanced at each other knowing they were about to be out-muscled. Adam started the climb. He was ten or so feet up when he stopped and looked down. Instantly he lost his grip and fell to the sand with a thud, providing the others amusement.

"Is that a piece of cake or humble pie?" Billy laughed.

"Shut up." Adam said, embarrassed. "And for the record, they're a great band." Adam stood up, his ego more bruised than his posterior. He shook off the fall, brushed off his pride, and jumped with bare feet back onto the trunk of the tree to try again.

Nestor offered another bit of advice. "Be patient. Be steady. One look down, one slip da hand, and gravity get you." But again Adam's feet slipped off the bark and he plummeted.

Tess stepped forward.

"Give it a rest, Adam." Looking to Nestor, "Can I go next?"

Nestor waved her on, and on her first try she made it to the top, where she looked down at Adam and flashed a wide smile. The others applauded Tess while she proudly shimmied her way back down. Adam kicked at the ground and headed over to sulk in the shade. The others took their turns reaching the top and touching the coconut, each smiling at Adam, who applauded them unenthusiastically.

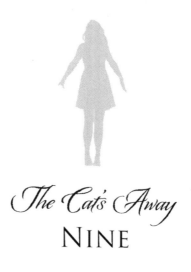

The Cat's Away

NINE

M ajor Conroy woke Carrie and Roger early on Saturday morning in standard military fashion. This was the day he and Joanna were leaving for Hawaii, and he wanted things to go by the book while they were gone. His drill instructor demeanor was designed to set a serious tone.

Roger was grumpy and wondered why they didn't just leave a note and go. Besides, on Saturday mornings Roger typically slept in till noon. Rubbing the sleep out of his eyes, he loaded his parents' luggage into the island's only taxi, which waited out front. Carrie slid onto the bench seat in the taxi next to Joanna and began to pull rogue blonde hairs off her mom's new black sleeveless sundress.

Joanna was excited, but nervous about leaving the kids alone. Major Conroy looked grimly at Roger and Carrie.

"Okay, kids, remember what I said—no messing around."

This was met by a sharp salute from Roger.

Joanna added, "We're relying on you both to take care of things. Take turns feeding Magoo and Snoop. And please don't forget, Maru needs to be on the last boat to Ebeye by six every night. Don't keep her late."

"We won't," Carrie assured her.

The four of them walked quietly down the tarmac to the aircraft until Carrie broke the silence.

"Don't worry, Mom, everything will be fine. Just have fun. Bring me back a lei or something, okay?"

Joanna smiled.

"I will, sweetie. Love you both. You kids be good."

The baggage handler took their bags and Carrie and Roger waved good-bye, all the while thinking "Hello" to their freedom. Joanna blew them a kiss as they disappeared inside the air-conditioned fuselage. It was all Carrie and Roger could do not to run back home jumping and cheering.

~~~~~~

The ocean water was warm that Saturday afternoon and Carrie's slalom ski cut through the water like silk.

Adam was observing in the back of the boat while Roger piloted. They circled a floating dock where Tess, Gina, and Billy waited their turns. The mice were at play, and the sunny, beautiful day was theirs to do with what they pleased.

Suddenly Adam pointed at something behind Carrie in the water. A fin barely breaking the surface not forty feet behind her had caught his attention. He shouted, "Oh, holy fuck! Don't fall down, Carrie!" Adam turned to Roger.

"Take us back to shore, Rog! Hurry!"

Carrie wanted to look back but was afraid she'd fall. Besides, it was clear from the look on Adam's face that something was not right. All she had to do was keep her balance and stay focused. Roger yelled, "Hold on, Carrie!" as he shoved the accelerator all the way forward.

Tess, Gina, and Billy stood on the dock, and when they realized what was happening, they all began yelling, "Shark! *Shark!*"

Roger looked back at Carrie to make sure she was okay. Adam screamed, "Faster, Roger! Get her into the shallow water!"

Roger nodded to Adam, but when he turned back, he saw a buoy right in front of them. Instinctively he quickly cranked the steering wheel to avoid hitting it, but Carrie's ski rope caught the buoy, yanking the rope out of her hands.

Adam stood up and yelled, "Oh, shit!"

Roger looked back, then pulled back the throttle and cranked the steering wheel. Carrie slowly sank into the water. Now she could clearly see a huge fin barreling right for her. She was frozen in terror as she bobbed up and down like a child's water toy about to be sucked into the skimmer. The ski boat abruptly divided the final ten feet between Carrie and the shark as Adam and Roger reached down and swept her up, pulling her into the boat.

Carrie shuddered uncontrollably in Roger's arms, as Adam watched the shark move out from under the boat and off into the distance. Adam looked at Roger and Carrie in disbelief. His face was as white as Carrie's. All they could do was sit quietly and try to catch their breath. Today, freedom had almost come with a very hefty price.

~~~~~~

A jet rumbled through the blue sky, leaving a white contrail in its wake. Inside the airplane Joanna squeezed Major Conroy's hand as he sipped on his second scotch. Joanna had a look of concern on her face.

"Do you think the kids will be okay?"

Major Conroy smiled at her.

"This isn't California honey. It's safe here. And, they're good kids. They'll be fine. Besides, I put the fear of God into them."

The Yuk
TEN

The Yuk Club offered the only fine dining on Kwajalein. It was a private club and popular haven for military personnel and their families. Next to the club entrance, a small sign was posted in the Marshallese language that stated:

No Marshallese Allowed on These Premises. Anybody Caught Will Face Imprisonment and Will Be Ruined.

Of course, the English-speaking residents had no idea what the sign said, but its message was loud and clear to the Marshallese. Apparently the sign had been written, and perhaps posted by a Marshallese who had been the unfortunate recipient of the wrath of the military's implementation of this local law.

Besides being the only restaurant and bar for the adults, weekends at the Yuk provided nightly entertainment, which had quickly transformed it into the island's hot spot. One of the favorite attractions was when Erita, the Tahitian dance teacher, would provide entertainment with her husband's band, Filet of Soul, featuring her students who had made it to performance level.

Carrie, Gina, and Tess had all made it. The three girls had started attending Erita's weekly dance class shortly after they had arrived on the island, and they were getting quite good. Carrie was fascinated with the storytelling of the dance and treated the traditional handmade grass skirts and cowry-shell headbands that Erita made for them like priceless jewels. The girls learned quickly that Tahitian dancing was more than just the shaking of hips and storytelling with the hands, it required real skill and lots of practice. You had to bend your knees, keep your shoulders very still, and create tight, smooth circles with your hips at a very fast speed. This would cause the red tassels on the band of the skirt to rise. The higher you could get them to rise while using the correct movements, the more skilled a dancer you were considered to be. It was a challenge that the three girls embraced.

As the evening was winding down, the small audience sat sipping navy grogs and mai tais while

Erita and the girls danced to the band playing popular Hawaiian songs. Filet of Soul's featured ukulele player, Mig, was a handsome twenty-four-year-old Hawaiian with deep brown eyes and Elvis-like hair. Carrie and Mig often exchanged smiles during performances, causing Carrie's insides to melt a little each time.

When the band's last number built to a crescendo, Mig held one hand in the air signifying the end of the song. A smattering of applause came from the small crowd and from a few military personnel who were hanging out at the bar. The girls and members of the band bowed, and then Mig said, "Thanks, everybody. We'll be back next week. Hope to see you then."

Mig left the stage and approached Carrie.

"Carrie, good job tonight. You girls get better every week."

Carrie lit up.

"Thanks, Mig."

Mig smiled, "You're welcome. Um, the boys and I are gonna head out. We've had a long day. See you at rehearsal."

Carrie was flattered that Mig was addressing her directly.

"Yeah, okay. Looking forward to it." She watched as Mig and the band packed up their gear and left the Yuk, secretly wishing that Mig would stay.

Lieutenant Ryan Mitchell, the officer Carrie had first met on the airplane, leaned against the bar, cocktail in hand. He was slightly buzzed, and by the way he was looking at Carrie, you could tell he was undressing her with his eyes.

Sergeant Derrick Anderson, Lieutenant Mitchell's sidekick, could almost hear Ryan's thoughts as Ryan studied Carrie's posterior.

"Easy, big guy. That's Major Conroy's daughter. You don't wanna shit in your own nest," he warned.

Ryan smiled, pushed himself away from the bar, and held up two fingers.

"I've done her, twice."

Derrick smiled and rolled his eyes at Ryan's comment. He watched Ryan cross the room and approach Carrie, as she and the other dancers finished up a glass of punch.

From behind Carrie, Ryan studied the charm bracelet on her wrist, baring the charm with her name on it. He broke into her conversation.

"So, Carrie, you're the girl with the umbrella, right?"

Carrie turned.

"Yeah. And you're the guy who told me it wasn't going to rain, right? How did you know my name, anyway?"

Ryan pointed to the name charm.

Carrie nodded, "Oh, yeah, I forgot about that."

"So how are you and your family enjoying the island so far?" Ryan asked, trying to make some light conversation.

"We really like it, thanks." Carrie said, quickly adding, "I've gotta go now and get changed." She turned and walked away.

Ryan shifted his attention to Donna, who was wearing a revealing, low-cut blouse and sitting at a table with Billy, Roger, and Adam.

Sitting by himself at a table in a darkened corner was Corporal Doug Jessie, drinking a scotch and rocks. Unbeknownst to Ryan and Derrick, Corporal Jessie was paying close attention to the behavior of his fellow officers.

Ryan sauntered a little unsteadily up to Donna's table.

"Excuse me, this might seem a bit forward, but I just wanted to tell you. Of all the girls on this island, you are definitely the most beautiful."

Donna was flattered and thanked him for the compliment, which encouraged his questioning. "What's your name?" Ryan asked.

"I'm Donna," she answered softly.

"I'm Lieutenant Ryan Mitchell, and I gotta tell ya, if I didn't know better, I would think you were a high fashion model or something."

This comment made Donna blush. Adam rolled his eyes and turned to Billy, who started to say something but held back at the last minute.

Sergeant Anderson held up a fresh drink at the bar and called out, "Ryan, your drink's up."

Ryan curtailed his conversation with Donna by saying, "It was nice meeting you Donna. Hope to see you again soon." He turned and headed back to the bar. It was clear from Donna's smile that Ryan's flattery had gotten him everywhere.

Corporal Jessie finished his drink, paid his tab, and exited the club. A few moments later, an old Marshallese man who was obviously intoxicated entered the club and steadied himself up against the bar.

Donna rushed over to Carrie, who had changed into her street clothes and was walking over to join the boys at the table. Pulling Carrie aside, she told her, "Carrie, see that guy over there, Ryan? He is sooo cute. He just told me he thinks I'm the most beautiful girl on the island."

"That's nice, I guess. Just be careful," Carrie said.

"Oh, I will," Donna replied.

Donna was floating on cloud nine and Carrie could see she was very taken by Ryan.

Ryan had just knocked back his third scotch when his eyes fell upon the old Marshallese man. Ryan leaned close to Derrick and said, "This should be fun."

He walked up and nudged the old man.

"Hey, think you missed your boat. You know better than to step foot inside here. You better get going." The man said nothing.

"Guess you didn't hear me?" Ryan chided. "I'll say it again. You better get going."

The old man mumbled something under his breath.

"What'd you say?" Ryan said a bit louder.

"You didn't lose your way, did you? Hard to imagine you'd get lost tonight, especially with this full moon out."

At that moment, Ryan pantsed the old Marshallese man, grabbing his trousers and pulling them down around his ankles. The old man quickly tried to regain his composure, but he lost his balance and fell to the floor. Both Ryan and Derrick laughed, deriving a great deal of entertainment at the old man's expense.

Carrie looked over at Donna as if to say, *This is the guy you like?* Carrie felt uneasy and was disgusted. She stood up and felt certain that somebody would come to the old man's aid. The reality that no one was taking action quickly sank in. Thoughts of the night Sara had died shot through Carrie's brain, abruptly causing her to get up and leave the Yuk Club. Carrie was sickened, realizing that she was again part of this silent majority.

On a Clear Day
ELEVEN

Gina had claimed her spot on the beach and was in the process of applying tanning lotion to her already bronzed legs when Carrie and Donna positioned their towels on either side of her. Carrie smoothed out the mounds of sand beneath her favorite beach towel, the one with the large red hibiscus flower. She made herself comfortable and then tied back her hair in a high ponytail. Donna hid her face under a striped sun visor that matched her blue and purple bikini and lay down flat on her stomach, asking her sister to join them. Tess wasn't in the mood to sunbathe. She'd come to the beach fully clothed. Often, Tess would compare lying out in the sun to being the equivalent of a chicken roasting in the oven. She loved being in the water, or sitting under the shade of a palm, but to just lie still and bake never appealed to her. She sat down near the others and applied a heavy smear of white zinc oxide to her nose, which she would reapply and wear during the day, the same way the other girls would apply and reapply their pink Bonne Bell lip-gloss.

Adam and Billy walked up with Roger limping close behind. It was obvious from the shade of red on their shoulders and foreheads that they had been on the beach for a good portion of the morning and early afternoon. Roger hopped on over and sat cross-legged on the sand next to Tess. He placed his right foot on his opposite thigh and, grimacing, began to pick something out from the bottom of his foot.

"Man, I really miss the sandy beaches in California. You didn't have to worry about this fuckin' coral reef tearing the shit out of your feet."

Adam said, "Actually I prefer coral reefer. Anyone holding?"

Roger scoffed, shook his head and said, "Adam, you're a hopeless pothead."

Roger asked the group, "Seriously, didn't you see the photo of that guy on the bulletin board at the Teen Center? His foot was majorly shredded."

Carrie seemed quiet, a little distant. It was as if she hadn't heard a word Roger or Adam had said. To no one in particular, she stated, "I just can't quit thinking about last night. I feel so bad that nobody helped that old Marshallese man." Hesitating for just a moment,

66

she twisted her Coke can in the sand, making a depression to hold it, and continued, "I would have liked to *shred* that Ryan guy."

Donna looked up, "I thought it was kinda funny."

Tess turned and looked at her sister incredulously.

"Wow, really, Donna? Sometimes I don't think I know you at all."

Tess looked over at Carrie.

"You know, you're right Carrie, we should've helped that poor guy."

Billy nodded in agreement.

"Yeah, we should have done something. Why'd we all just sit there anyway? My brother Ted once told me, the hottest places in hell are reserved for those who in a crisis, do nothing."

Everyone sat silent, but their expressionless faces spoke volumes. Gina seemed agitated and consumed in thought. She slowly got up from her towel and walked off toward the water. Billy joined up with her and put his arm on her shoulder as they continued walking down the beach.

Donna watched them go. She didn't really know what she felt about Ryan. All she knew was that he was nice to her, and he thought she was beautiful. Maybe what had happened at the Yuk with the Marshallese man was a one-time thing. She certainly hoped so.

As she continued to watch Billy and Gina walk down the beach, she spoke her thoughts out loud, pointing.

"That's my dream right there. I just want to be walking on a beach somewhere with someone who loves me. You know, really loves me, not just for what I look like, but for who I am."

Tess was still irritated by Donna's callous remark about the Marshallese guy, but she *was* her sister and knew how vulnerable and gullible Donna could be sometimes.

"You will, Donna. You'll find someone new. That other guy was a jerk, anyway."

Adam looked up at this comment.

"What happened?"

"It's a sensitive subject. She doesn't want to talk about it," Tess quipped.

Ignoring Tess, Donna charged right in.

"There was this guy in school that I really liked. He told me he loved me, and I believed him. We finally slept together. I wouldn't have done it, but I really thought he might be the one. Right after that, he dumped me, and I found out he only slept with me on a bet. God, you can't even imagine how embarrassed and humiliated I was. I was completely crushed. I didn't think I could ever step foot on campus again."

"So, how much did the guy win in the bet?" Roger asked sarcastically.

Donna was appalled at the wise-ass remark. "Funny. Asshole." she replied.

Tess threw a handful of wet sand at Roger.

"Fuck you, Roger." Turning to Carrie, she said, "Carrie, your brother's a dip wad."

Adam wanted to get going. He'd had enough beach time and was ready to head over to the fourth hole and grab a beer. He asked the rest of the group if they were ready to go, and the others couldn't get up and ready fast enough. Adam shouted down the beach to Gina and Billy, who were barely within earshot.

"We're going to the fourth hole. You guys coming?"

Billy looked at Gina, who just shrugged. It was apparent she would much rather spend some one-on-one time with Billy. He shouted back to Adam.

"Go on ahead, and we'll meet up with you guys later."

Walking back over to their bikes, a light bulb seemed to go on in Roger's head.

"Hey, that reminds me. We should have a party this weekend at my house. My folks are gone till the sixteenth. We have the place all to ourselves."

Adam smiled, "Yeah, far out. Party at the Conroy's."

~~~~~

It wasn't much longer than an hour or so before Gina and Billy joined the others at the fourth hole. They were two beers behind. Gina didn't feel like drinking and she wanted to go over to the Teen Center and get out of the sun. Carrie and Tess agreed to ride over with her, and the boys indicated that they would meet up with them a bit later. Billy put a quarter in the beer machine, got his can of Olympia, and sat down behind the Quonset hut with Adam and Roger. He gave Gina a grin and waved good-bye as the girls rode off.

The wind felt good on Carrie's face and she could feel the slight sting on her sunburned cheeks. As they rounded the bend, the marina came into full view, and the boats all seemed to bob up and down in the gasoline-laden water, creating little psychedelic circles of color around them.

Carrie stopped her bike suddenly.

"Is that Mig down there? What's he doing?" she asked. It looked like him, but she wasn't sure. He was bent over, working on something, and all she could really see was his shiny black hair.

"I think that's him." Gina said.

"I know he has a boat cuz my dad mentioned that he had worked with him a time or two. He's a scuba diver. Does some kind of work for the military. I can't remember what, though."

"He is so cute," Carrie said dreamily, and they could hear in her voice that her interest was more than just casual.

Tess looked over at Mig.

"Carrie, you got a crush on that old guy? Not only is he too old for you, bachelors are strictly off-limits. Speaking of crushes, Gina, what was up with you and Billy at the beach today?"

Gina blushed a bit.

"I'm not sure how it even happened. It just kinda crept up on us. I can't explain it."

Tess wanted to get going, but Carrie wasn't ready to go. She wanted to take this opportunity to talk to Mig alone.

"You guys go ahead," she said, without taking her gaze off Mig.

"No. Don't even think about it. All you're doing is asking for trouble," Tess replied, sounding irritated.

Carrie ignored the advice.

"I'll be fine, worrywart. I won't be long. I'll see you guys in a little while."

Tess huffed in frustration.

"Fine. Be that way." She rode off and Gina followed close behind.

Carrie parked her bike near the dock and walked slowly down to the boat. She could hear a loud rumbling noise coming from a compressor inside the boat cabin. Mig turned quickly, sensing someone behind him, and was surprised to see Carrie standing there.

"Hi, Mig!" she said. "I didn't know you had a boat."

Mig quickly relaxed and smiled at Carrie.

"Yeah, it's my work boat, part of what I do for the military. Nose-cone recovery after a rocket launches and stuff like that."

Carrie scrunched up her nose, "I'm not really sure what that means, but it sounds cool." She loved the idea that he was a scuba diver. It was something that she was too scared to do, even though a lot of the people on Kwaj seemed to take advantage of the opportunity to learn and get certified.

The compressor shut off abruptly.

"I'll be right back. I need to disconnect my scuba tank," Mig said, and went inside the cabin.

Carrie waited for him. She knew it was a long shot, but she wanted to invite him to the party. Mig emerged from the cabin and joined her on the dock. Carrie said quickly, "Hey, we're having a party at my house over the weekend. I'd love it if you could come." She held her breath, hoping he would say yes.

Mig paused for a moment before speaking, eyes shifting around.

"Ahh, that's probably not the best idea. But I do appreciate the invite."

Carrie looked sad, and Mig could see that he had just stolen the wind from her sails. But when she looked away from him, he saw her eyes brighten and rest on a beautiful *Tonna* shell that he had sitting on his console. It was one that he had retrieved during a dive not long ago and it was a real beauty.

Carrie brought her attention back to Mig. Not wanting to show her disappointment, she asked in an upbeat voice, "Are you going to be at the Rich Theater for the movie next week?"

Mig wasn't sure, but he didn't want to let her down twice.

"I hope I can make it, but it depends on my work schedule."

Carrie gave him a smile, and surprised herself by kissing him on the cheek. Mig stood straight as an arrow, completely caught off guard. Carrie couldn't believe what she had just done and she ran off, nearly knocking over Rudy, Mig's Japanese diving partner, who was approaching the boat. Carrie jumped on her bike and waved at Mig as she rode off with her insides shaking.

Rudy cocked his head and shot Mig a look. Mig shrugged, "Hey, don't look at me like that. I know she's way too young. Besides, nothing is going to happen. It takes two to tango, you know."

Rudy continued to glare at him.

"That's what I'm afraid of."

Execution Island

TWELVE

Just a few blocks away from the Berkeley campus was the Steppenwolf Pub, where many students studied, or so they said. A long-haired, bearded hippie stood out front on the sidewalk next to a stack of underground newspapers called the *Berkeley Tribe*. He waved one of the newspapers to passersby. "Get your copy right here!"

A college radical named Brian approached the pub and grabbed a newspaper from the stack, quickly scanned it, and walked inside. Ted sat at the bar wearing an American flag sleeveless shirt, as he poured a cold beer into a glass. As Brian passed the bar, he held up the newspaper and said, "Hey, Ted, did you see the R. Crumb cartoon in the *Tribe?*"

Ted replied, "Yeah, hysterical, huh? That guy nails it every time."

Brian agreed and then added, "We got a good turnout for the rally on Friday."

Ted smiled over his shoulder.

"Right on, man. Thanks, Brian." He grabbed the duffel bag next to him and retrieved a book entitled *Takin' It to the Streets*. A couple of photos fell onto the bar from the bag and into a puddle of condensation. Ted quickly dried them off, stopped at one, and smiled. The old dog-eared photo was of Billy and him posed together at the Grand Canyon. The other photo was a current picture of Ted at a peace rally wearing a peace sign armband. He set this photo aside. He put the one of Billy away in his duffel bag before pulling out a sheet of blank paper and a pen. Billy was Ted's link back to normality, just as Ted was for Billy. Ted missed his little brother. He wished they could be fishing together in a mountain stream like the old days. College and war protests had consumed Ted and he could feel the loss of connection from his former self. This troubled him, although just this subtle awareness made Ted want to stop everything and reopen up that line of communication with Billy. Ted tapped the pen on the bar as his thoughts turned to his little brother Billy and what he wanted to say to him. Ted knew Billy looked up to him a great deal, so he chose his words carefully and started to write.

The bartender switched the channel from football to news and lowered the volume. Footage of the Vietnam War began to play. Fighter-bombers dropped napalm, and troops moved through heavy jungles, carrying wounded.

Ted began the letter.

Hey Spud Boy,

Just wanted to shoot you a quick note and catch you up on things. Berkeley is great. However, lots of classmates have been looking to me lately to lead this charge on the anti-war movement. I kind of feel it's an honor, but I'm getting way more attention than I'd like.

Jennifer's been staying with me while she's looking for a new place. Included is a picture of me at one of our rallies wearing a peace sign armband that she made for me. Pretty cool, huh?

I hope you're making new friends there and settling in. Did you get the protest flyers I sent you? Don't want you to get in trouble but I think the message is pretty important. Maybe spring break we can meet up stateside and go on a camping trip together. My buddy Brian knows this lake just outside of Fresno that has amazing trout. I know you're dying for a chance to out-fish me. (although it will never happen little man!) Let me know how things are going on Kwaj, and say hi to Mom and Dad for me. And as they said at Woodstock, watch out for the brown acid, Spud Boy.

Love, your brother,
Ted

Ted looked up. On the TV a crowd of protesting students held signs that read *Burn Your Draft Cards*. Ted lifted his glass of beer and gave a toast to his allies on the TV screen.

~~~~~~

At Kwajalein High, Mr. Bachman's history class was under way and Billy had just finished reading his letter from Ted. For Billy, getting a letter from Ted was rejuvenating and exciting. Billy looked at the photo Ted had sent him, smiled, and put it away.

Carrie and her friends all had the same third-period history class. Mr. Bachman, their teacher, was forty-three and considered to be cool by most of his students. Mainly because he was a fan of all the bands who had played at Woodstock, and they knew that if he were twenty years younger he'd be letting his freak flag fly. He carried his permanently wrapped right arm in a sling that covered his hand, as well.

Mr. Bachman said, "Okay, I liked your reports. You'll get them back tomorrow, graded."

Adam interrupted.

"Hey, Mr. Bachman, can Billy talk about his report to the class? He was telling me about it, and it's really far out. I think everyone would like to hear it."

Mr. Bachman hesitated.

"Well, I guess so." He asked Billy, "Do you want to talk about your report with the class?"

"Yeah, sure. Okay." Billy got up and walked up to the front.

"Well, I wanted to do my report on something that was historically accurate about Kwaj, since we all live here. I was talking to my dad, and he told me about a time before World War II when the Japanese were still in control here. The Japanese had taken Marines prisoner and had intended to ship them to Tokyo. Then they were advised not to and were told they could just get rid of them however they saw fit.

So, to celebrate some Japanese holiday, they decided to behead them all."

Several of the students gasped. Billy continued, "Yeah, freaky, I know. Anyway, that got Kwajalein a nickname, which became the name of my report—Execution Island."

Gina looked around at the stunned students, raised her hand, and said, "Wow, hard to imagine such a horrible thing happening right here in the middle of paradise. Spooky."

Roger replied, "Yeah, well, at least I know what I'm gonna be for Halloween now—the Ghost of Execution Island."

Mr. Bachman rolled his eyes as several students laughed. He was glad the discussion had ended on a lighthearted note despite the delicate subject matter. It might have been a part of history, but it was very close to home.

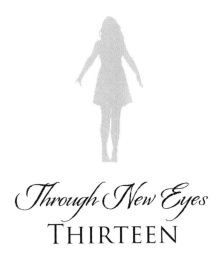

Through New Eyes

THIRTEEN

From outside the Conroy house, The Rolling Stones' *Gimme Shelter* could faintly be heard coming from inside. A reel-to-reel tape machine tracked the music as Roger monitored the sound with headphones on, adjusting the audio.

In the bathroom, Carrie, Tess, and Gina were busy putting their makeup on for the party as they danced and sang to the music around open beer bottles surrounding the sink.

Carrie dipped her makeup brush in some blue eye shadow and looked away from the mirror and over at the girls.

"This is gonna be so much fun tonight. I mean, when is the last time we got to party with no parents around? It's like we have our very own place!"

Tess let out a whoop, "No kidding. Can you imagine how fun it will be when we have our own apartment? The three of us living together, roomies, that would be so bitchen."

Carrie looked back in the mirror, "I can't wait. No rules, doing whatever we want, seeing whomever we want. Hey Gina, what time do you think Billy's coming over?"

Gina just shrugged, "I don't know, I don't even know if he's coming. I haven't heard from him in days. What about Mig? Did you ask him?" she inquired, as she continued to apply her eyeliner.

Carrie replied, "Yeah, he's not coming. I really wanted him to, but he told me he didn't think it was a good idea. I was really hoping that I could..."

At that moment Maru peeked her head in to say goodnight. "I catch boat to Ebeye now."

Carrie realized she still needed some help to get things ready.

"Oh, Maru, wait. Could you do one thing for me? We're having a party here tonight." She added, "My parents said it was okay." Carrie turned to her friends and rolled her eyes before turning back to Maru.

"And we could really use some punch, and maybe there's some stuff here to make sandwiches or something?"

Maru nodded and said, "Yes, Miss Carrie."

Roger began hanging black-light posters over his mother's seascapes. Maru checked the clock in the kitchen as she walked by with a monkey pod punch bowl. The clock read 5:25. Gina poured ice into a large bucket and Tess filled it with beer bottles. Maru set out the bowl of punch, then checked the clock again and quickly began preparing some sandwiches. Carrie fed the pets while Gina covertly poured a fifth of vodka into the punch bowl. The clock now read 5:40.

Maru rushed out the tray of sandwiches she had prepared and set them on the table. She glanced up at the clock and her face fell. It was now 6:05. Carrie walked in and saw Maru's expression, then looked at the time and realized what had happened.

"Oh, no, Maru. I'm so sorry. I made you miss your boat!"

Maru just stared at the clock, knowing how promptly the boat left every night, and said in a monotone voice, "Yes, I miss boat."

Gears quickly turned in Carrie's head as she took Maru by the hand and sat her down.

"Maru, don't worry," she said. "This is what we're gonna do. You will come to the party, and then you can sleep here tonight."

Tess and Gina walked in and instantly knew something was up. Maru just shook her head and said, "No, I no come to party. I must leave island."

Carrie knew the Marshallese couldn't stay on the island past six o'clock, but what could she do?

"Yes, yes, you can. It's okay, and we'll get you something to wear, and we'll do your hair and your makeup." Looking up at Tess and Gina for support, she asked, "Won't we, guys?"

Tess nodded in agreement, "Yes, of course. Maru, it will be fun!" Gina raised her eyebrows and added, "Yeah, no problem."

Maru managed a nervous smile while Carrie and the girls led her to the bathroom.

Jimi Hendrix's *Foxy Lady* blared through the house as Maru got her makeover. Carrie applied her makeup, Tess was in charge of hair, and Gina fitted her in a red sundress. The final result was to be revealed to Maru in a full-length mirror in Carrie's parents' bedroom.

"Ta dah!" Carrie exclaimed, when they had finished. The girls escorted Maru, with her eyes closed, down the hall into the bedroom and positioned her in front of the mirror.

Carrie said, "Okay, open your eyes." Maru's expression was somewhere between shock and wonder. Maru leaned in and looked closely at her face in the mirror. Her eyes had been shadowed with a shimmery blue, her cheeks were a rosy pink and her lips, a luscious shade of red. A huge smile quickly won her over as she saw herself through new eyes. She turned and hugged Carrie so tightly that Carrie though she might pass out. Maru looked beautiful.

Carrie exclaimed, "Maru, look at yourself! You look so pretty!" She placed a tube of red lipstick in Maru's palm and wrapped her fingers around it.

"This is for you. To keep."

Maru turned and gave the other girls a hug, as well.

"Thank you so much," she said. Carrie was brimming with pride. She was so pleased that things were coming together, despite the Maru hiccup.

Mice Will Play
FOURTEEN

The reel-to-reel was playing Three Dog Night's *Mama Told Me Not To Come*. Twenty-five or so kids filled the Conroy home as they danced in a haze of smoke and partied in psychedelic strobe lighting. Adam, Donna, and Billy arrived with more beer in hand to support the cause. Carrie caught Maru collecting empty beer bottles and emptying ashtrays.

"Maru, stop that! You're not a maid tonight. Roger will do that." Roger heard this and shot Carrie a death glare.

"Yeah, Maru, come out on the lanai with me and Donna," Gina said.

Gary, a classmate, stopped Donna on her way out.

"Hey, you here with anyone tonight?"

"Whaddaya mean? A date? No," she replied.

"You want to go slip off and make our own party somewhere?" he offered.

"I've got some good weed."

"I don't think so, Gary. I'm having fun. I'm gonna hang tight. Thanks anyway," Donna said with a smile.

"Hang tight?" Gary said.

"That's the opposite of what I heard *you* were."

"Huh? What's that supposed to mean?" Donna snapped, realizing the implication of his comment.

"You know, loose. Open for business. That's the word around school, anyway."

Donna pulled her hand out of her pocket and flipped him a downward finger.

"If you can't hear this, I'll turn it up for you." She pointed her middle finger upward. "Go fuck yourself, Gary!"

Donna was crushed. She headed for the front door as Gary wisecracked, "Geez, wish I could, but I was kind of hoping you could help me with that." Donna slammed the door behind her.

As Donna exited Carrie's house, she felt diminished and dirty. This wasn't something she could easily dismiss. When Donna had arrived on Kwaj, she had started with a clean slate, and Gary had just sullied it.

In the backyard on Carrie's lanai, Billy, Gina, Adam, Maru, and Tess were standing in a circle, passing a joint. Maru watched Adam pass it to Billy, who took a big hit off it and then passed it to Tess. "'ere," Billy said.

Tess did the same and passed it to Maru, who hesitated but then shrugged and imitated the others. She took a huge hit, coughed, passed it along, and said, "'ere." They all laughed, and Maru wondered what was so funny.

Later Roger brought out a handful of bottle rockets that he had kept stashed in his closet.

"Who has matches? I got a bunch of fireworks for a song from this Marshallese kid on Ebeye."

Adam found a book of matches in his pocket and handed them to Roger. They began lighting them one by one in an empty beer bottle they had placed in the sand. Billy began to build a small fire with driftwood.

As the fireworks exploded in the sky, the party seemed to thin out, leaving Carrie, Maru, and Carrie's small circle of friends. They were all seated around the fire, and Adam joined the group, saying, "Man, I wish we had more of those bottle rockets, Rog. That was fun."

"Yeah, well, I have some more but hate to use 'em all tonight. Who knows, we might be pushing our luck. Don't want Curtis coming down on us."

Laughing, Adam said, "Curtis, what a dork."

"Speaking of rockets, I heard they're gonna shoot off another one here at the end of the month," Gina said.

"Really?" Carrie asked. "I hope it doesn't fall back on the island this time."

"Let's look on the bright side. If it does, maybe it'll fall on the school," Tess joked.

The group laughed, and Carrie took another drink and finished off her beer.

"That was so scary," she said.

"Yeah, that was nuts," Adam agreed, shaking his head.

Gina speculated that it was probably just a satellite or something, but she wasn't sure.

Billy piped up.

"Satellite? They don't launch satellites from Kwaj. It was probably a nuke."

Adam smirked.

"A nuke? Right. If that was a nuke that slammed into the ground at the Teen Center, we'd all be dust."

Billy shook his head.

"I don't know what it was, man. All I know is that this base is where they test nukes sometimes. That's what I've heard."

Carrie pulled on her sweatshirt.

"You think that's true?"

"They wouldn't allow us to live here if it was dangerous," Adam insisted.

"Well, according to my brother, they've tested nukes all around this area for years," Billy said.

A moment passed before Tess chimed in.

"Well, why are we living here then?

Billy looked at her for a long moment before commenting, "That's a really good question."

His comment made the group grow silent, and they stared into the fire, watching the driftwood crumble into a pile of hot, orange coals.

~~~~~~

Two MPs pulled up to the house, walked up to the front door, and knocked. They could hear the music, but there was no answer at the door. One of the MPs peeked through the front window and saw what he thought was a Marshallese maid in a red dress walk by through an open doorway. They headed around back to find the kids sitting on the beach by the dwindling fire.

"Excuse me, are your parents home?" one of the MPs inquired. Carrie and Roger both stood up quickly, and Carrie responded, "Um, no, they're in Hawaii right now."

The same MP nodded.

"I see. Do you have fireworks in your possession?"

Carrie hesitated, "Well, we had a few, but they're gone now. We don't have any more."

She looked over at Roger, "Do we?" Roger assured the MPs that they had fired off the last of them.

The MPs reminded the group that fireworks were illegal on the island and so were fires on the beach. They instructed the kids to put out the fire, which they agreed to do right away. Roger apologized, telling them he was on it, not wanting to give them any reason to hang around. He had sobered quickly and knew that this could be trouble with the amount of alcohol and weed they had on hand.

The MP told him to make sure to put it out completely and then addressed Carrie.

"Do you have a Marshallese maid in the house?"

Maru and Gina were just about to come outside when they heard the MP's question. They froze like statues behind the curtain.

Carrie felt a little panicky but tried to remain calm.

"Uh, no. Why?" she asked.

The MP looked doubtfully at Carrie.

"You sure? Wearing a red dress?"

Gina acted quickly and ran Maru into the back bedroom.

The MP was still talking to Carrie.

"If you do, we'll have to take her in. It's well past Marshallese curfew. No domestics allowed on the island after six o'clock. We're gonna need to search the house."

Timing it perfectly, Gina strolled outside, wearing Maru's red dress.

The MP looked at her and seemed puzzled.

"Oh, sorry, our mistake. Um, you kids just get this fire put out and make sure you don't light off any more fireworks, okay?"

Carrie felt a rush of relief.

"Yes, sir, officer. We will. I mean, we won't."

The MPs turned and left, and Carrie exhaled in relief. She grabbed Gina's arm and pulled her close, whispering in her ear.

"Thanks, you saved my ass."

The next morning, Carrie stepped over several sleeping bodies on the floor and entered the living room, which was sparkling clean. Maru stood there smiling in her maid outfit, still wearing the bright red lipstick from the night before.

"I clean." Maru beamed.

Movie Night
FIFTEEN

The Richardson Theater was popular with the Kwaj kids, and tonight was no different. It was a great place to turn on, tune in, and drop out. Since the island was under military law, there was a strict adherence to rules and regulations, and that included what the military thought was appropriate viewing material for the theater. As a result, the movies shown at the Rich were less than desirable, featuring entire seasons of *McHale's Navy* that had been transferred to film, science movies, a select few holiday films, and random cartoons.

Billy and Gina sat watching another rerun of *McHale's Navy* at the Rich. Ever since the party at Carrie's house, Billy had become preoccupied with the mysteries of the military presence on Kwaj, and he wouldn't let up.

Billy whispered to Gina, "I asked my dad about what exactly they do here on the base, and he got all weird about it. Ya know, if they don't have anything to hide, what's with all the secrecy and nobody talking? Do you know—"

"Billy, enough," Gina said, cutting him off. "Watch the movie."

"Gina, this is important shit I'm talking about," Billy said as he leaned forward in his seat.

Gina folded her arms and replied firmly, "I just wanna watch the movie."

"Fine. Whatever," Billy said flatly.

Inside the projection booth lived the projectionist, Scout, who was eighteen and smoking a joint. Scout had hoped to be a film major back on the mainland, but Kwaj High offered nothing even close. Scout figured this was as good as it was going to get while he served his time out on the rock. Besides, the booth had an exhaust fan that worked great to cover up getting high, and this made it a cool hang for those in the know. A shelf unit against the back wall was full of film canisters of all sizes. Scout enjoyed being at the Rich, even though the selection of films was pretty bleak. It was his home away from home.

There was a knock at the door, and Adam and Billy entered. Adam took a whiff of the sweet aroma and said, "I thought I saw smoke in here."

"Entrez," Scout said, and he handed Adam the doobie.

Billy saw the rack full of films.

"Wow, look at all these movies. Cool. Hey, Scout, do you have *Butch Cassidy and the Sundance Kid* in here?"

"Dude, are you kidding? We get nothin' but shit," admitted Scout.

"How 'bout *Easy Rider?"* Billy asked.

"Ha! I wish."

Adam handed the joint back to Scout when he noticed something in the theater through the projection glass window.

"Is that that Ryan guy sitting with Donna?"

"Yeah. What is she, like sixteen?" Scout said. "Guy's a perv, if you ask me. And worse yet, I heard he has his sights set on Carrie—she's even younger. That's messed up, man."

Adam shot Scout a look of disbelief.

"Are you shittin' me?"

Billy was insistent.

"How 'bout that freaky one? You know, *Rosemary's Baby?"*

Scout was becoming annoyed with Billy's inquiries.

"Dude, no."

Adam was still looking through the window.

"If that dude wasn't the General's son, his ass would be so kicked off this island."

"I know," Scout said.

"The Wild Bunch. Do you have that one?" Billy tried again.

Scout laid into him.

"Billy, do you really think I'd be showing fucking *McHale's Navy* if I had *The Wild Bunch?* Really?"

While the movie was playing, Donna got up and slipped out through the side exit, hoping to be unseen. A few minutes passed before Ryan got up, made a quick visual scan of the theater, and then exited through the same door.

The moon was almost full as Ryan left the parking lot in his father's car. Donna arrived home on her bike and quietly snuck in the back door so as not to be noticed. She sat nervously on the edge of her bed, fidgeting. A few moments passed before she heard a faint tapping on her bedroom window. She rushed over and opened it and Ryan climbed in and immediately began kissing and fondling her.

"Slow down," she said in a whisper.

"I'm kinda nervous."

"Yeah, me too," he replied pulling out a flask.

"So I brought this to help us relax." He turned to close the window but noticed that across the street, Mig was riding up to Carrie's house on his bike. Ryan watched, transfixed, as Carrie greeted Mig on her front porch.

Carrie was surprised to see Mig at her house. He seemed a bit awkward as he glanced around and fumbled for his words. He handed Carrie the *Tonna* shell that she had admired on the day they had talked at his boat. Carrie's face lit up and a thousand feelings all at once surged through her.

"Mig, thank you so much. How did you know I wanted one of these?"

"I saw you looking at it the other day when you were down at my boat. I had a feeling you would like it," he admitted.

"Wow, it is so cool. I started a shell collection, you know, but I only have a few. This is by far the best one of all. I love it!"

Across the street in Donna's bedroom, Ryan secretly watched as Carrie gave Mig a big kiss on his cheek. He then saw Mig turn and leave Carrie's house. Ryan, taking this in, slowly turned back to Donna as she switched off the light.

Carrie admired the *Tonna* shell as she went back in her bedroom. She placed it on her bookshelf with the other, much smaller shells she had found on the beach at low tide. It was by far the biggest and most impressive shell in her collection.

Carrie looked at herself in her dresser mirror and smiled as she brushed her hair. New thoughts and feelings replaced the little girl crushes and hopeless fantasies that she knew were merely adolescent pipe dreams. The look in Mig's eyes had been so telling, she thought. It was somehow different from what she had seen before at rehearsals or down by his boat.

Oh my God, she realized. This was not a one-sided crush anymore, this was real. She picked up the shell again and held it close to her. She couldn't help but feel that the size of it, compared to the other shells, somehow represented how much Mig felt for her.

She placed the shell on top of her dresser with her most sentimental keepsakes and pictures of her friends. She was wide-awake now, and her mind was alive with excitement and wonder. She wanted to scream as loud as she could, but it would surely wake the entire family and bring them streaming in. At that moment, Magoo jumped up on her windowsill, and she ran excitedly and opened the window, letting him in.

"I love you, Magoo!" she said as she picked him up, showering him with hugs and kisses. She began jumping and dancing in circles around her room, much to Magoo's chagrin.

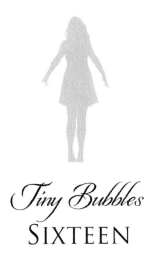

Tiny Bubbles
SIXTEEN

Mig tuned his ukulele while the rest of the band set up for the upcoming rehearsal with Erita and the girls. Carrie, Gina, and Tess walked into the Yuk Club, laughing and nudging one another. Upon seeing the band they quickly became quiet, as if protecting some private joke or island gossip.

Mig looked up and smiled.

"Aloha, girls. Hey, Carrie, did you bring the cassette recorder? I was hoping you could record the new song today."

"Got it right here," she said, retrieving it from her bag. Mig had asked her at last weeks practice if she could bring it to all future rehearsals. Carrie, wanting to be helpful and to show Mig how reliable she was, had gone straight home and put it in her dance bag so as not to forget.

Mig smiled at Carrie.

"Great."

He reminded the girls that their next performance was on the twenty-second and asked if they thought they would have the new dance moves down by then. Gina quickly said that she didn't think it would be a problem and turned to Carrie for corroboration. Carrie was fiddling with the machine. She looked up, agreed with Gina, and told Mig that as long as they had the music to practice with, there was no need to worry. Pressing a button, she looked down at the red light on the machine.

"Okay guys, we're recording."

The girls took their places on the stage. Mig messed with his dark hair, combing it forward with his fingers and letting it hang heavy over his eyes. Looking like Elvis but speaking with a heavy English accent, he said, "I'd like to say thank you on behalf of the group and ourselves, and I hope we pass the audition."

Everyone laughed, and Carrie laughed the hardest of all. Mig had done his John Lennon impersonation many times before, and it never got old. In fact, to Carrie, it got better each time.

Mig continued, "And that Carrie and the girls come to all the rehearsals instead of Yoko."

Carrie felt a rush of affection sweep through her. She adored him. Mig looked at the band and began to count off: one, two, three, four. The band broke into Don Ho's rendition of *Tiny Bubbles,* with Mig singing lead.

The girls' graceful hands poetically told the story of love and intoxication as their wheat-colored grass skirts swayed in perfect synchrony. The girls always enjoyed dancing the occasional hula, as it was much more relaxing and much easier for them than the traditional Tahitian dances that made up the majority of their performances.

Mig's voice was deep and smooth, and when he sang the lyrics, *With a feeling that I'm gonna love you till the end of time*, Carrie couldn't help but look him directly in the eye. Mig saw the look and returned it with a smile. Carrie was sure that she wasn't imagining it, and she felt he really was singing the song to her.

So here's to the golden moon, and here's to the silver sea. And mostly here's a toast to you and me. So here's to the ginger lei I give to you today. And here's a kiss that will not fade away.

Several songs later, the bass player praised both the band and the girls and told everyone to take a short break. Mig put down his uke, took a drink from the glass of water he kept on a nearby stool, and then walked off toward the bathroom. Carrie watched as Mig headed down the hall, and though she knew she shouldn't, she couldn't help but follow him. She saw him enter the bathroom, and Carrie wasn't sure what was coming over her, but she felt an urgent need to see him now, alone.

Before he could close the door behind him, she managed to push her way in, slam the door shut, and lock it. Mig was completely startled.

"What in the world are you doing, Carrie?" His expression turned to one of deep concern. Carrie didn't know what to say, so instead she just grabbed him and pressed her lips hard against his. Mig instinctively pushed her away.

"Stop it, Carrie. This cannot happen. Please, leave."

He saw a look of disappointment fall like a curtain over her face, the same look he had seen when she had come down to the dock and he had refused her party invitation. He felt horrible, but this was so inappropriate, so dangerous.

Carrie, speaking under her breath, pressed on.

"I don't get it, Mig. Why did you come over the other night? Why did you bring me that shell? I thought it was because you liked me. I mean, why else would you come over?"

Mig was overcome with guilt, realizing that he had indeed been sending mixed messages. He now knew that it had been a bad idea, one that could only lead to trouble. He looked at a confused Carrie as she waited for some response.

"You know, I guess I shouldn't have, but I saw you admiring the shell, and I really wanted you to have it," Mig explained.

Carrie tried again. "But Mig, I *really* like you."

Shaking his head, "I like you, too, Carrie, but this is just not right. My God, you're fifteen, and I'm twenty-four. We could get into serious trouble."

Carrie grabbed Mig's hand and placed it firmly on her right breast.

Surprised and a bit shaken, he quickly pulled his hand away. "Carrie, stop. Please don't do this."

"Can't we at least talk about it?" Carrie pleaded. "How about if I come over to your place a little later?"

Mig took a step back, "At the barracks? Absolutely not! The barracks are off-limits, you know that, and if we were to get caught, we would both be kicked off this island. Now, come on, Carrie." Mig gave her a pat on the arm and then pushed past her, opened the door, and looked both ways before he exited the bathroom.

Even though Carrie had been rejected, she knew Mig wasn't being honest with himself. She had seen it with her own eyes. She saw the looks, she heard it in his voice, and she knew for a fact that he really liked her. He had come to her house and brought her that beautiful shell, he had given her a gift! And she had kissed his lips. Even though he'd pulled away, she knew he didn't want to. She felt it through her entire being, penetrating all the way through to her bones.

Called Out on the Carpet
SEVENTEEN

The military base was active on Monday morning as Lieutenant Ryan Mitchell and Sergeant Derrick Anderson approached the Base Commander's headquarters. The Commanding General was Ryan's father, and this relationship offered its share of perks, including serving out his tour on Kwaj, not to mention circumventing front line activities in Vietnam, risking life and limb.

The General's clerk, Corporal Doug Jessie, sat across the desk from the General and as he could sense the Commander looking at him, he looked up. "Yes sir?" The General leaned back in his large, brown, leather chair and clasped his hands behind his head. "Corporal Jessie, I trust that not having heard anything from you, means that our esteemed Lieutenant Mitchell has been behaving himself off base?"

Corporal Jessie appeared caught off guard by this as he rose. There was a sense of code and loyalty amongst the officers and Corporal Jessie honored this. Willfully dishing up dirt on an individual would position one as a brown-noser or a rat, which came with its own set of consequences.

"Um, yes sir, for the most part, he has sir."

The General looked over the top of his bifocals, paused and said, "*For the most part*? What does *for the most part* mean Corporal? When I give a directive, I expect specifics. When they inquire why you lost three years of seniority and why your off-base privileges were revoked, I'll just say, well, *for the most part,* Corporal Jessie was a-okay."

Corporal Jessie cleared his throat and backpedaled, "Perhaps there was something sir..."

Down the hall, double doors careened open as Lieutenant Ryan Mitchell and Sergeant Derrick Anderson walked in unison down the hallway. You could almost hear a marching snare drum that matched their perfect stride as they moved down the waxed, linoleum hallway, their patent leather, standard regulation, polished shoes keeping perfect military time.

Corporal Jessie began to speak while the General stood and turned to gaze out his office window. As Corporal Jessie relayed the events he'd witnessed at the Yuk Club, the General's eyes seem to glaze over. Memories of Ryan when he was a young boy at Wade Military Academy swam through his head. It was a memory the General couldn't forget, although he wished he could.

Ryan had been twelve at the time, and the General and his wife were called into Wade for a conference. They came to a door marked Henry L. Cultler, Col., USMC President, Wade Military Academy, and entered. Inside Ryan sat with a lost look on his face across from a large antique desk where the uniformed Colonel Cultler sat. The Colonel rose to greet the General and his wife as they entered. Handshakes and pleasantries were exchanged, and then the Colonel got directly to the business at hand, namely Ryan.

"Wade Military Academy has a standard of ethics expected of our cadets that, regretfully, we feel has been compromised by your son, Ryan. Several cadets witnessed him exposing himself during Basic Cadet Training last Thursday. An Honor Board's jury has determined that Cadet Mitchell has violated the code and has been recommended for sanctions for this violation. Unfortunately, this particular sanction will result in Cadet Mitchell's disenrollment from Wade Military Academy, waiving the violator's right to be placed on a probationary status."

The General nodded and looked over at Ryan, eyes reflecting his disgrace and disappointment. Ryan's dismissal from Wade had come a year before he would have graduated.

~~~~~~~

Lieutenant Ryan Mitchell and Sergeant Derrick Anderson approached Staff Assistant, Sheila Davis. She smiled and motioned for them to enter. After shutting the door behind them, Ryan and Derrick stood at attention and saluted. General Mitchell directed them to be at ease. Sergeant Anderson spoke. "Sir, the USS Pennsylvania is en route, and we have confirmed its arrival for Thursday, sixteen hundred hours."

The General got up to look at a calendar on the wall behind his desk.

"Very good, Sergeant. Thank you. Dismissed."

The two of them turned to leave, but the General, glancing at Ryan, knew there was unfinished business that had to be dealt with.

"Lieutenant Mitchell, I'll need a word with you."

"Yes, sir," Ryan replied as he searched his mind for what this could possibly be about.

Ryan's father turned to his assistant, Corporal Doug Jessie.

"Can you excuse us for a moment, Corporal?" Corporal Jessie saluted and replied in the affirmative, leaving them alone in the office.

The General instructed Ryan to sit and did so himself. The General leaned forward in his chair and folded his hands in front of him.

"Information has crossed my desk that you were seen several weeks ago over at the Yuk Club fraternizing with some of the young high school girls," he began. "I don't want to have this conversation with you, son. I'm just a tad busy here running an anti-nuke program. I've got a live warhead out there, locked and loaded, that I just might have to use at any moment to take out a Russian missile heading towards us at over fifteen thousand miles an hour. And frankly, I don't have time to deal with any of your sexual shenanigans."

The General rose to his feet and leaned over his desk. In a tone that Ryan only heard when his father was deathly serious, he said, "Don't disgrace me again, Ryan. Because, if you do, I will have your sweet little candy ass sent to the front lines. You'll be eating out of a can, shitting in the jungle, and rubbing elbows with those gooks so fast, your shaved little head will spin. Do I make myself clear, son?"

Ryan cleared his throat.

"Um, yes, sir."

"Good." The General sat back down, turned around in his chair to stare out the window and dismissed him. Ryan saluted the back of his father's head, turned, and exited the office.

Sixteen Hundred Hours

EIGHTEEN

M ig and Rudy descended into the lagoon where a derelict ship lived in the shadows. This was an ongoing scuba diving directive they had been assigned to when they weren't doing nose-cone recovery for the missile test facility.

It was a tireless job involving the underwater salvage of small craft that the military could possibly reuse or that just needed to be moved and disposed of. Sometimes they would have to clear shallow obstructions, like masts, off of deeper, bigger ships. All in all, it seemed never-ending. Many of the military aircraft and sea vessels were left in the Kwajalein lagoon after World War II. Most were stripped and scuttled, but a few were still armed and considered active. Not the safest job on the island, but someone had to do it.

Taking up their flashlights, slowly they moved inside the silt-laden ship and carefully inched their way down into an ammunition room. Mig found the artillery hold and got Rudy's attention to photograph its contents. Large unexploded shells, still in their huge, rusted magazines, lay dormant.

Suddenly a grouper fish that had to be well over six feet long appeared behind them. Startled, Mig turned and reeled back, slamming into the bulkhead and causing silt to explode everywhere. The two of them pushed beyond their zero visibility and left the vessel as fast as they could, staying ahead of the cloud of silt that would consume them if they lost their forward momentum.

As they exited the ship, a large shadow moved over them. On the surface, the USS Pennsylvania rumbled by, headed for the Kwaj military base.

The Kwajalein military personnel hustled as the USS Pennsylvania docked and began offloading a large container marked with a radioactive hazard symbol. Lieutenant Ryan Mitchell oversaw this operation. It had to be a coordinated effort to safely deal with offloading a container that housed the volatile nuke head that was to be the focus of a coordinated launch between Vandenberg Air Force Base and Kwaj at the end of the month.

A huge crane lifted the container onto the platform, and several crewmen approached it with hydraulic ratchets and removed the lug nuts at its base. A moment later the container shell was safely lifted, revealing the military's latest model in nuclear efficiency, the Zeus anti-missile nuclear warhead.

Do You Smell Smoke?
NINETEEN

After a long five-hour flight, Major Conroy and Joanna's C-130 military transport, touched down on the Kwajalein airstrip. Joanna was relieved to be back. As much as she had enjoyed spending time in Hawaii, her mind had never truly left Kwaj and had stayed right at home with her kids, never allowing her to fully relax.

Major Conroy removed his reading glasses, rubbed his eyes, then folded up his *Honolulu Star* newspaper and tossed it on the empty seat across the aisle. Joanna placed a bookmark midway through Jacqueline Susann's novel *Valley of the Dolls*, which was the only part of the flight coming to an end that she regretted.

When she had first started reading it, she instantly hated it. She felt dirty just seeing certain words, felt guilty for even being curious about the characters' lives, possibly because of her good Catholic girl upbringing. But she quickly became absorbed and concerned about the characters, and, heaven help her, she couldn't put it down.

She hated that Neely was such a bitch and that Anne could be so haughty. It was trashy and entertaining, and she had tried to hide the book cover so that others didn't know what she was reading. She somehow felt that associating with these fictional characters, even if only by reading about their drug abuse and reckless lives, was a reflection of her, an indication of her own moral compass or, worse yet, something she longed for.

Snapping back to reality, she quickly ran a brush through her hair, applied a fresh coat of lipstick, and stuffed everything back into her carry-on bag, anxious to get home to her normal little drama and sleeping pill–free life.

Carrie and Roger heard the taxi pull up out front and ran out to greet their parents. Joanna stepped out, put her suitcase down on the ground and hugged Carrie as hard as she could. She lifted a beautiful braided lei of fragrant white pikake flowers and small pink and white orchids from around her neck and placed it over her daughter's head.

Carrie breathed in deeply.

"Aww, thanks, Mom." Kissing her mother's cheek, she asked, "Did you guys have fun?"

Joanna assured her that they had had a great time but were happy to be home. Carrie picked up her mother's suitcase and they all walked into the house, where Snoop wiggled around and excitedly greeted the foursome.

Tossing her bag on the couch, Joanna bent over and reached into it. She pulled out a jar of macadamia nuts and handed them over to Roger, asking, "So, did everything go okay here?"

"Yeah, Mom, everything was cool. Thanks for the nuts. I love these." He twisted open the sealed jar and tossed a salty handful into his mouth.

Joanna was already busy tidying up the front room, putting the little knick-knacks back in order, the way she had left them.

"So, no problems? I'm guessing everything was okay and Maru made it to the boat each evening on time?"

Magoo appeared and began to meow, rubbing his head up and down and leaving a tri-colored sweep of hair on Joanna's pant leg. She bent down to scratch him behind the ears.

"Hello Magoo. Well, it looks like the animals were well fed."

Carrie told her that everything had gone great. No problems at all. And, believe it or not, she and Roger never even had a fight! Joanna looked around the room and wrinkled up her nose.

"Does it smell like smoke in here?"

Roger and Carrie quickly and nervously replied in unison with a big "No!" and gave each other a look of solidarity, a private signal to one another that they were on the same page, part of the same team.

Just at that moment Maru walked through the room wearing the uncharacteristically bright red lipstick Carrie had given her. She gave a toothy smile to Joanna.

"Hello, Miz Conroy. Nice see you."

Joanna smiled at Maru.

"You too, Maru." She looked over at Carrie, scrunching up her face in confusion, and mouthed to her, "What's with Maru?" Carrie just shrugged, feigning ignorance, but inside her giggles were hard to contain.

"Anybody home?" Donna called out as she opened the front door and entered the house without knocking.

"Hi, Mrs. Conroy. Welcome back."

Joanna was just heading off down the hallway to the bedroom to unpack her suitcase, "Oh, hi, Donna. How are you, honey?" Not waiting for an answer, she again wrinkled up her nose.

"God, I swear it smells like smoke in here. Donna, do you think it smells like smoke in here?"

Donna seemed edgy, a little nervous.

"No, I don't think so." She quickly turned her attention to Carrie. "Can I talk to you?"

"Yeah, sure." Carrie picked up her cat, Magoo, and led Donna to her bedroom. She shut the door behind her and they both sat down on the edge of Carrie's bed. Donna sat quietly, her hands together in her lap, fidgeting with the little jade ring she wore on her right hand. Carrie waited patiently for her to begin talking; she could tell that whatever Donna wanted to say was difficult for her.

Donna swallowed hard.

"You're not going to believe this, but I *have* to tell someone. I'm really scared." She looked up from her hands and with a hint of fear in her eyes continued, "Well, I don't even know where to begin. But I know I can trust you."

Carrie nodded but stayed silent, waiting.

"Oh, God, Carrie, my period's late. I think I might be PG!" Donna pressed the palms of her hands hard against her forehead. Carrie sat there straight-faced and speechless. Donna wasn't sure what she had expected Carrie to do or say, but she needed *something* from her.

"I don't know for sure, but I just feel really different, you know? God, what am I going to do? I'm not ready to have a baby! My parents are going to kill me." She began to cry.

Carrie was still taking in this unexpected news, it had stunned her like a swatted fly and she couldn't quite get a handle on it.

"What in the world are you talking about? How can you be pregnant? You haven't even been seeing anyone." Carrie questioned.

"Oh, please, promise me you won't tell a soul." Donna held her breath for a moment and then blurted out, "I slept with Ryan."

"What?!" Carrie couldn't believe her ears. She didn't know what she was feeling, whether it was shock, surprise, or disgust. She couldn't believe that Donna would be so stupid and so careless, and she couldn't hide her repulsion.

"Ryan? Ryan Mitchell? No way! I told you he—"

Donna didn't let her finish.

"I know, Carrie! This isn't the time for your I-told-you-sos!"

Donna felt bad enough as it was. Maybe coming to Carrie wasn't the best idea, but she had needed to tell someone. She knew that if she shared this with her sister, Tess, all she would be given was grief; and Gina, well, Gina would have acted like it was no big deal. She was scared, and now she looked it.

"All I know, Carrie, is that I don't want to get kicked off the island."

Carrie felt bad and a bit ashamed of herself. She knew that she had reacted harshly, when what her friend really needed at this moment was a friend, not a judge and jury. Carrie took Donna's hand in hers.

"Are you gonna tell Ryan?"

She squeezed Carrie's hand hard.

"I think I'm gonna have to."

Rude Awakening
TWENTY

Donna was trembling inside. Even though she had unloaded her burden and shared the news with Carrie, she still felt an overwhelming feeling of helplessness, of being completely alone. She needed to talk to Ryan, and there was never going to be a good time. She would tell him today. Maybe he would be excited. Maybe this would be the happiest day of his life. Donna let the fantasy play out in her head for a few minutes: the two of them, happily married with a baby.

She tried hard to gather the courage to confront him, and the only way she could do this was to believe that this was meant to happen, that they were meant to be together. This was God's will.

Donna knew that going to the base might not be the best move, but it was the only sure way she had of seeing him, at least anytime soon. She approached the guard shack with an air of determination, convincing herself that she had every right to be there. The guard was at his post, watching her as she came closer.

"I'm here to see Lieutenant Ryan Mitchell, please. It's very important."

The guard knew better than to bother Lieutenant Mitchell, especially with something that was obviously a personal matter, but he could see that the girl was troubled, and he didn't want to turn her away. Besides, it just might add some entertainment to the guard's routine day.

"I'll page him for you, but I'm not sure where he is on the base, so I can't guarantee you he'll hear it." He spoke into the loudspeaker. "Lieutenant Ryan Mitchell, please report to the guard shack. Lieutenant Ryan Mitchell, report to the guard shack."

Several minutes went by and Donna's nerves were starting to get the best of her. She paced back and forth, and she began to panic as she felt the speech she had memorized slipping from her mind.

Catching her off guard, Ryan came up behind her and grabbed her by the arm. He seemed annoyed.

"Donna, what in the hell are you doing here?"

Donna turned abruptly, facing him, her throat tightening.

"I need to talk to you."

"Jesus, Donna, you know I'm on duty. This isn't a good time." Ryan was agitated.

Her heart sank. This wasn't how she wanted him to react upon seeing her. But the hurt instantly gave way to frustration, and he was going to listen to what she had to say.

"Oh, really? I'm sorry if it's not a good time for you, Ryan, but I'm pregnant!"

Ryan quickly looked over at the MP in the guard shack. The MP busied himself, and if he had heard anything, he knew better than to let on.

Grabbing her arm again, a little bit tighter this time, he said, "Shhhhhhh! God, be quiet. We can't stay here. Come with me."

He led her away from the guard post and out next to the maintenance building, where his father's car was parked. Ryan opened the passenger door for her to get in and then walked around, got in the driver's seat, reached under the front seat for the keys, and started the car. He sped out of the parking lot but then caught himself and slowed down. He definitely didn't need to attract any unnecessary attention. He looked over at Donna, who sat staring straight ahead with her hands tightly clasped together in her lap.

"What were you thinking, coming to the base and making a scene like that?" Ryan shook his head, as if implying that what she had done was an act of complete stupidity.

She continued to look straight ahead.

"I wouldn't really call that a scene, Ryan." She turned to look at him.

"I'm sorry if it's not convenient for you that I'm pregnant!"

Donna didn't know where this inner voice was coming from, and she didn't quite understand it, but something much bigger than her was handling this situation.

Ryan tapped his fingers forcefully along the steering wheel, as if to some loud music playing in his head. Or perhaps he was trying to stomp out the mental chatter of his father's stern message, warning him of the consequences of any further indiscretions. This was certainly something Ryan did not need; this wasn't part of the plan. All he had wanted was a little fun, a good time. He couldn't look at her. In a deadpan voice he asked.

"You sure it's mine?"

All her resolve vanished, and she couldn't hold back her emotions.

"Oh my God, Ryan, you're the *only* guy I've slept with."

Ryan knew he had to play it cool, not upset the apple cart. He couldn't risk anyone finding out about this, and he needed to do whatever was necessary to ensure exactly that. He would think of something, but for now he just had to convince her that everything was going to be okay. He needed her to trust him. He looked at her as she wiped her nose and dabbed at her eyes.

"Okay, okay, sorry. I had to ask. Let me think for a few minutes."

Donna turned to him, "I'm so scared, Ryan. And you know I'll be kicked off the island and have to leave all my friends. I'll have to live with my grandmother. She'll be so ashamed of me."

Ryan arrived at the beach and pulled the car over. He got out and went around to help Donna. He hoped that no one would go by and see the General's car. That would be all he needed, he didn't want to have to answer to his father about that.

Taking Donna by the hand, he led her down to the water. Looking her in the eye, he spoke slowly and clearly.

"Look, I'm not gonna let you go through this alone. I'm here for you. But this is the deal. *Nobody* can know that I'm involved in this, or I'm screwed."

Donna had settled down a bit and was hanging on to Ryan's every word. He continued, "You might get sent off the island to go live with your granny, but if anyone finds out I'm involved, I'll get sent to the front lines or maybe even worse, go to jail. And then you *will* be on your own. I don't want that, Donna."

He took her face in his hands and, with a look of devotion, spoke to her lovingly.

"How 'bout this? I've only got a few months left in my tour. As soon as I finish, I *promise* I'll fly back and do right by you and the baby. It won't be long. And as soon as I get there, we'll get married."

Donna lit up like the firework finale on the Fourth of July. Her imaginary life wasn't going to be imaginary after all. Giving him a rib-breaking bear hug, she buried her head in his chest and breathed in his goodness.

"Oh, Ryan, I love you so much. And I promise you, I won't say a word to anyone."

Off-Limits
TWENTY-ONE

The bachelors' barracks were strictly off-limits to civilians. These orders were firm and very well known throughout the island.

Even though Carrie was well aware that a pregnant Donna had already received her official walking papers and would be leaving the island shortly, Carrie somehow felt exempt. All she knew was that she had night's cloak on her side, and nothing was going to keep her from her Romeo.

She stealthily emerged from the shadows and darted across the driveway, slipping quietly up to the entrance of the barracks. Carefully twisting the doorknob, she opened the main door and slid inside. It wasn't until then that she realized she had no plan for finding Mig's room. But she had to find him, and she had to do it quickly. At any moment, someone could exit one of the rooms or enter the quarters, and she would have some serious explaining to do and might end up on a one-way flight off the island.

Moving slowly down the hallway, she kept a keen eye out in all directions. Then she noticed nameplates over the doors, sparking a sigh of relief. She quickly scanned them until she found the one marked MIG KAPULA. She immediately entered the room without knocking.

Mig was stretched out on his bed, reading a diving magazine and listening to Hawaiian music when she came in. Startled, he bolted upright, astonished to see her.

"Carrie, what are you doing here?" Mig quickly pulled his curtains closed. He wasn't the kind of person who took risks or disobeyed the rules. Even as a kid he rarely got in trouble, unless he was late for dinner because the surf was up and he couldn't pull himself away from the ocean. But this was a blatant disregard for strictly enforced rules. It could mean a dishonorable discharge, or at the very least, a transfer off the island to a desk job somewhere he would undoubtedly hate. Whatever the outcome, it wouldn't be good, and he knew it.

Carrie saw Mig, smiled, and rushed over to him. She was seemingly oblivious to the peril she was subjecting them to, but she didn't care. She was with him and that was all that mattered.

"I'm sorry, but I really need to talk to you. I don't think you know how much I feel for you. And I know you feel something for me too, don't you?" Carrie said as she sat down at the foot of his bed.

Mig knew he had to set Carrie straight. He sat down next to her and took her by the shoulders.

"Of course I do. I like you, Carrie. But this just isn't right. You are so young, and I am much too old for you."

But Carrie didn't feel that age mattered. Blinded by her emotions, she only knew that she had feelings that couldn't be denied. It was as if love had given her a "get out of jail free" card and she was somehow impervious to society's rules and regulations. She was here in his room now. She could smell his aftershave, and it activated something deep inside her that she had never felt before. Her intentions were strong, and the longing to be in his arms was overpowering. Every ounce of strength she had to resist him was rapidly collapsing in on itself and she felt herself sliding toward him. Carrie leaned in and began kissing him.

At first Mig was taken aback by this, but it was already happening, and he felt himself kissing her back. His resistance weakened. He embraced her. He took her into his arms and pulled her close to him. Carrie hadn't expected this, which only caused her to surge with even more passion. She was so happy that she felt as if she would explode inside.

A hundred thoughts of why this was wrong raced through Mig's head but were quickly thwarted by feelings he had kept at bay. Notions of a little-sister fondness were quickly dismissed and abandoned as passion and desire dominated Mig's consciousness. His mouth opened almost simultaneously to hers, and they fell back onto his bed and time stood still. Somehow they had found each other here, on this tiny island in the middle of nowhere, and love had found them, too.

Beside Mig's bed, the hula girl lamp holding his puka shell necklace stood like a sentry watching over them as soft Hawaiian music filled the room.

Then, across Mig's wall, a wash of white light streamed in from the headlamps of a car pulling up outside. Mig quickly got up and peeked out the window. He saw Ryan getting out of his father's car and approaching the barracks. Carrie eyed the puka shell necklace draped over the lampshade, quickly grabbed it, and put it on over her head. Mig spun around and with an urgent whisper said, "It's Ryan! You have to go."

"Ugh, that creep. He got Donna pregnant, you know. Don't tell anyone." She was up and had shifted gears in her head to survival mode.

"Really? You're kidding." He opened his door for her. "Hurry, Carrie, go out the back so Ryan won't see you."

Carrie knew there was no time for a good-bye kiss, and she slipped out into the hallway. She could see Ryan stepping up onto the porch now. She bolted down the hall to the back door and moved quietly outside. As Ryan entered the barracks, the sound of the back screen door closing caught his attention. He looked up and clearly saw Carrie pass by the window and descend the back steps. Immediately he put two and two together and went directly into Mig's room.

"What the hell do you think you're doing?" Ryan said.

"What are you talking about?" Mig shrugged as he slid the Hawaiian record album back into its sleeve.

"I just saw Carrie Conroy leave here."

"What?" Mig said incredulously. Ryan scanned the room. Simultaneously their eyes fell upon Carrie's charm bracelet, which had fallen off onto the bed. Mig winced as Ryan quickly snapped it up and dangled it in front of him.

"Not only could I have you kicked off the island, I could have you arrested right now and charged with rape."

Mig began to pace.

"Okay, Ryan," he admitted. "She showed up uninvited. That's the truth. I told her to leave, and she left. Nothing happened."

Ryan cocked his head.

"You think I was born yesterday, you fuckin' moke?"

"Think whatever you want, Mitchell. But I'm not the one getting young girls pregnant around here."

Mig's words stopped Ryan on a dime.

"What the fuck are you talking about?"

"I know about you and Donna. You got her pregnant. Maybe you should be taking your own advice," Mig said, standing his ground.

"You got a lotta fuckin' nerve!" Ryan grabbed Mig by the throat and slammed him up against the wall, sending a framed picture of Mig and his surf instructor to the floor, shattering.

Mig used this moment to land a solid connect to Ryan's midsection, doubling him over, and he followed it by slamming him across the nose. Pain shot through Ryan's brain and his eyes began to water. Blood began to run down Ryan's wrists as he held his nose and cursed at Mig. Suddenly the door burst open, revealing Nestor and startling them both.

"Hey, what's going on here?" Nestor yelled, standing akimbo in the open doorway.

"Nothing," Ryan replied, picking up his hat while still holding his bleeding nose. "We had a disagreement. It's over."

Ryan forced his way past Nestor and exited the room. Nestor looked at Mig, whose adrenalin was still pumping. Mig just shook his head as if to say, *Don't even ask.*

Ryan entered his room and went into the bathroom to examine his bloody nose in the mirror. Pulling some toilet paper off the spool, he dabbed it. Not only did it hurt, but what was worse was that the cat was out of the bag about Donna. His eyes darted around the bathroom, and he could feel his world spiraling as he heard his father's speech echoing through his head. Visions of being on the front line, dodging napalm and death, exploded through his brain like a mortar shell.

"God dammit!" he shouted as he punched his reflection, shattering the mirror.

~~~~~~

The next morning a Marshallese cleaning woman finished vacuuming a room and moved to the bed, which she began to make. As she tucked in the sheet between the box spring and the mattress, she stopped at an obstruction and slowly pulled out a hidden magazine entitled *Men's Night Out,* featuring oiled, muscle-toned men on the cover. The maid nervously looked around, quickly replaced it, and finished making the bed. She turned and made her way into the bathroom and let out a large gasp. Over the sink was the shattered mirror Ryan had punched the night before. She shook her head and swept up the broken glass. She then emptied the trash, wiped down the sink and toilet, and exited the room with her cleaning cart. She closed the door, erasing from her mind what she had seen, and moved on to the next room.

Sabotage
TWENTY-TWO

It was hard to imagine such a beautiful day, so bright and sunny as this one. The air was so clear that you could see several neighboring islands peppering the horizon like a string of humpback whales. Seen through a pair of binoculars, Mig's boat rocked quietly in its slip at the dock, with no sign of Mig.

Strolling casually down the dock as if taking in the beautiful view, the visitor made a hard left turn and disappeared into the cabin of Mig's boat. Mig's air tank was next to an air compressor, and on the side of it were instructions for filling an aqualung with compressed air.

A gold class ring from Nutley High School with a red stone adorned the ring finger on the visitor's right hand, which he quickly covered with a pair of white cotton gloves. He picked up the air tank and began connecting it to the compressor.

Next, the instructions called for the compressor to be turned on and the tank filled, but they cautioned that the exhaust should be well ventilated. The exhaust vent was already positioned next to a window in the cabin, which was cracked open to allow for the ventilation. The gloved hands carefully closed it. An off-on switch was set to the "on" position, and the compressor rumbled to life. The valve on the tank was opened and it began to fill.

The visitor left the cabin and closed the door behind him, allowing the cabin and the tank to fill with the deadly carbon monoxide mixture. It reached capacity and shut itself off. Holding his breath, the visitor let himself back in, disconnected the aqualung and replaced it, and then reopened the vent window, leaving everything as it had been.

~~~~~~~

By the time Mig had arrived at the boat, Rudy had already organized their scuba equipment for the morning dive. Kwajalein possessed some of richest communities of corals and fish on the lagoon pinnacle reefs, particularly those that got washed by tidal currents during the twice daily rising and falling tides. The lagoon, particularly around the southern part of the island and the northern island of Roi-Namur, was littered with the wreckage of war ships. They were mostly Japanese ships, sunk in the days leading up to the American invasion of the atoll in 1944. There were also many American aircraft, particularly in the north, scuttled after the end of the war.

On light days, shipwreck diving was normal for Mig and Rudy. Within just a few minutes Mig and Rudy had started their descent. They set their watches, switched from snorkels to regulators, and started letting air out of their buoyancy compensators to slowly begin their direct descent. Dropping in a totally controlled manner approximately sixty feet and looking around, they gently approached the bottom of the reef not twenty feet from a scuttled shipwreck.

The visibility was seemingly endless on this day, and the reef was alive with its usual inhabitants. Groupers, soapfish and butterflyfish were among the more conspicuous occupants. There were colorful males mixed in with larger groups of less colorful females. Some were fairly large and slowly wandered in and out of the shadows, sometimes catching the refracted, filtered light streaking in from above. Puffers and boxfish lurked about, mixing in with the many different species of triggerfish that divers were likely to see on any given day on this breath-taking Kwajalein reef.

Rudy was about six yards off Mig's right side. A large, beautiful basket shell caught Mig's attention.

They mostly stayed within the mucky sediments inside sunken ships and emerged at night to feed. Mig grabbed for his camera but in doing so, a thought, telling him he needed to leave and go to the surface flashed through his head. Quizzically, he looked at Rudy and wondered why he would have such a thought. Mig became acutely aware that he was breathing underwater—like the fish—not a worry in the world.

Rudy noticed that Mig seemed interested in the basket shell, and after his close examination and snapping a few pictures off, Mig lifted his head back up and actually started swimming toward Rudy. Mig appeared quite normal until Rudy looked back and saw Mig's regulator dangling and realized Mig was actually 'breathing' the water. Rudy's initial thought was that Mig was trying to say something to him, as they had done so in the past by mouthing words to each other under water. But Rudy thought Mig was 'talking' too long, so he swam over and put Mig's regulator back in his mouth. Mig immediately let it drop back out. Rudy then noticed a look in Mig's eyes that said, *Help Me,* sending a shock through Rudy's body. Rudy immediately grabbed Mig and started for the surface, while trying to get him to accept his regulator. A sudden uncontrollable fear and anxiety consumed Rudy but he knew from his training this would often lead to wild thinking and instantly calmed himself down to handle the situation.

Rudy was petrified of Mig embolizing. On a normal breath of air taken at sixty feet, you could gently exhale all the way to the surface and never run out of air. He also knew that the air must be expelled from your lungs in order to keep the capillaries in your lung tissue from rupturing, which would allow air bubbles to leak into your blood stream. Those tiny bubbles would continue to enlarge as you moved toward the surface, and the next thing you knew you would be dealing with a very serious diving emergency that even a decompression chamber sometimes couldn't reverse.

Mig's mask filled up with yellow slime and he was conscious that he was breathing water, but it rang no panic bell inside him nor did it tell his brain anything special. It wasn't a bad feeling at all. It doesn't take carbon monoxide long to do its damage and Mig had fell victim to it's deadly and sleepy intoxication.

On the surface, he could feel soft hands and the murmur of voices, sounding far away—nothing being said in particular. He heard his name being spoken far, far away. More murmurs. More soft hands.

"Mig, *MIG*!" Rudy yelled. Mig strained to open his eyes but they were so very heavy. Mig closed his eyes and could feel the soft hands touching his arms again. He could hear his name being called. Someone saying, "Mig, wake up!" Mig thought, *I'm so tired, just let me sleep.* There was no confusion inside him, just a very calm feeling.

Mig now heard new voices, more muffled conversation. A new feeling of hands on him—gentle, but not so soft. Rudy was still calling his name, telling him to wake up. Now, for the first time, Mig felt a slight twinge of confusion. A cold feeling surged through his body as it started to tremble. Someone was telling him to stay awake. But it was SO hard. Every part of his body began shaking, harder and uncontrollably. A blanket was placed over him and he was aware of someone removing the long pants he was wearing to protect his legs from the coral. Mig's last thoughts organized in his brain. *I just want to go to sleep. I'm not the least bit concerned. I'm not the least bit scared. I'm not the least bit worried. I'm not the least bit curious. I'm just shaking and I'm so very, very tired.*

Q With No A
TWENTY-THREE

Mr. Bachman's high school history class was full of inattentive and restless students on Tuesday morning. Carrie could see Mr. Bachman's mouth moving but didn't really hear his words, as her mind kept replaying her visit to Mig's room. Sitting at her desk, she could smell his warm, spicy cologne, all wrapped up in their kiss, she was consumed with thoughts of him.

Gina sat pushing back her cuticles, while Adam doodled Picasso-esque female figures on his paper bag book cover. Billy sat slumped down in his seat, his legs outstretched into the aisle, as he stared out the window at the rainbow-colored peace sign flag that flew faithfully outside Mr. Bachman's open door.

Mr. Bachman placed a bookmark in the book he had been reading from and slammed it shut, causing such a loud bang that everyone looked up at him and the busy chalkboard background.

"Okay, so that's the assignment. Any questions?"

Tess raised her hand.

"I have a question, Mr. B, but it doesn't have anything to do with the homework assignment."

Mr. Bachman lowered his glasses to the tip of his nose and peered over them.

"That's okay. Shoot. What's your question?"

Tess hesitated for a moment, but she had been bothered with all of this confusing talk about nukes, and who better to ask than Mr. Bachman?

"Well, I was just wondering—actually, we've all been kind of wondering—do they test nukes out here?"

Billy quickly interrupted, "Yeah, good question. Do they? My brother Ted told me they dropped A-bombs all over this place, and he knows what he's talking about—he's heavy into the anti-war protests at UC Berkeley. And I wanna talk about Vietnam, too."

Billy couldn't help but think about his brother Ted and all the work he was doing stateside trying to end the war in Vietnam. It was a fucked-up war and one Ted had told him that *no one* should be fighting.

Mr. Bachman glanced up at the clock on the wall.

"We can talk about Vietnam later, Billy. And to address your question, Tess, what they do out here is classified stuff. I'm not really at liberty to teach about things outside the specific curriculum that I've been given. And this subject is not part of this year's history course. I don't think we should get into it."

Billy challenged him, "Come on, Mr. B, World War II isn't history?" He sat there, his eyes fixed on his teacher.

Mr. Bachman wished he could share everything he knew and everything he had been through. They deserved to know how the world worked, what really went on, what the price of freedom was, and who was truly made to pay. He had become so close to these kids, and he was so damn fond of every single one of them. If he could draw a line in the sand, abide by certain boundaries, this would be much easier. He loved teaching them and wished he could cover anything and everything, but that wasn't the way the system worked. He wasn't authorized to venture into other areas or times in history, and he had been given a strict, preset lesson plan. Deviating from it could put his job in jeopardy, and then he wouldn't be able to teach them about anything at all. It was a lose-lose situation.

The other students sat in silence, waiting for Mr. Bachman to answer.

"Well, yes," he said. "That's true. What exactly do you want to know?"

Billy was a bit irritated by Mr. Bachman's evasiveness.

"Just give us some details. I mean, seriously, we're all wondering if this is a safe place for us to live."

Mr. Bachman twisted his mouth, bit his bottom lip, and chose his words carefully.

"I'm sure we wouldn't be here if it wasn't safe, Billy. Remember, kids, this *is* Kwajalein missile range, and they do test missiles out here. I mean, your parents all work here—you must know that."

The bell rang and the students all got up to leave. Billy wasn't satisfied with Mr. Bachman's answer and he rose to his feet slower than the others, taking his time to gather up his things. Mr. Bachman turned back to the blackboard and began erasing the heavy white chalk notes and diagrams from the day's lecture. He could feel Billy standing there, his eyes boring a hole through him, but he didn't want to engage. He could not get into this. He felt helpless, like a traitor, and as much as he would have liked to turn around, instead he continued to wipe down the board until he knew that Billy had left the class and the room was empty.

Dark Daze

TWENTY-FOUR

Carrie and Gina sat side by side in the faded red Naugahyde booth at the snack bar with a large plate of fries between them. Carrie dipped a few in the mound of ketchup, putting them all in her mouth in one big bite.

Donna walked over to the table, balancing a tray that supported a bowl of fried rice, a large Coke, and an order of pepper steak for Tess.

"Thanks, sis," Tess said and grabbed her plate from the tray while Donna squeezed in next to her.

Carrie seemed a bit upset and nervous.

"Hey you guys, have any of you seen my charm bracelet? It's gone and I have no idea what happened to it. I *never* take it off."

The girls shook their heads. None of them had seen it.

"Wow, I didn't even notice you weren't wearing it, which is weird, cuz it's such a part of you." Tess said as she grabbed her fork.

"No really, you guys. I'm sick about this. If I lost it, I don't know what I'd do. My sister gave it to me, you know."

The girls all told her they would be on the look out for it and not to worry. Between all of them, they would find it.

Carrie felt a small amount of relief.

"Okay, thanks, you guys."

She then held a fry between her thumb and forefinger and pointed it at the sky.

"Hey, do you guys think Billy really knows what he's talking about? I mean, about the nukes and all that? I can't imagine anything like that happening out here."

Tess put down her fork. She had been thinking about it a lot, especially after Bachman's class, when she had brought up the subject but left frustrated with little more information than when class had started.

"I know. What I don't get is, do you think our parents would really bring us to live in a place that wasn't safe?"

Gina had grown a bit tired of Billy's preoccupation with war and nukes, and frankly it was beginning to bore her. She had thought they might really have something between them, but everything seemed to change rather quickly. He didn't seem to have time for her. Gina had tried to act cool about the whole thing, like she didn't care, but she did. She wasn't accustomed to rejection and it hurt.

"Yeah, I don't think anything's going on here. I think it's just Billy overreacting. He seems to do that a lot lately. I don't think we have anything to worry about."

Carrie thought about what Gina had said. She was probably right, they should just let it go. And besides, what she really wanted to talk about was seeing Mig last night.

She blurted out, "Not to change the subject, but I went and saw Mig at the barracks." She didn't have to wait long for the reactions to come pelting in like the hailstorm that she had anticipated.

Tess jumped in first.

"What?! Carrie, are you fuckin' out of your mind? You went to the barracks?"

Carrie had expected nothing less from Tess.

"I know, kinda stupid. But I had to see him. I know you guys might think this is crazy, but I really think I'm in love."

By the looks on her friend's faces she knew what they were thinking, and she could tell they weren't taking her seriously. She was sick of people assuming that because you were young, love wasn't real, that it was a crush or puppy love, or something else less legitimate.

Gina eagerly inquired, "Tell us what happened. Fill us in."

Carrie's face turned about the same shade of red as the booth that she was seated in.

"We talked, and… we made out." Just saying it, felt almost as exciting as when she was actually doing it.

As the other girls oohed and aahed, Donna had been quiet, disengaged, but she needed to put in her two cents. Now that Donna had confided in Ryan about her pregnancy and she felt happy and excited about her future, she worried that Carrie might not be so lucky. Mig might not be the man that Ryan was. She looked down at her plate, picking the overcooked carrots out of her fried rice, and cautioned, "Carrie, please be careful. Don't do anything stupid."

"Looks who's talking," Carrie started in.

Just then, Preston Redding, a high school senior and the yearbook editor, burst through the snack bar entrance.

"Hey, does anybody know what's going on down at the marina? When I was riding up, I heard one of the old fishermen outside say there's an ambulance and a bunch of people down there."

Shrugs went around the room, and no one seemed to know anything. Carrie looked at the other girls; without even speaking, they all quickly got up and ran out, jumped on their bikes, and headed down to the dock.

At the marina, a crowd of people had gathered, and there was a lot of commotion and scurrying around. An ambulance was parked nearby with the back door wide-open, stretcher ready, and there was lots of undirected noise and yelling. A sense of disaster was in the air, a heaviness that closed in on the girls, lodging in their chests, making it hard to breathe.

Carrie eyed the ambulance and the crowd surrounding Mig's boat, then frantically threw her bike to the ground and began running in a panic down toward the dock. Ryan was standing near Mig's boat when he looked over his shoulder and saw Carrie headed his way. He didn't want her there—he didn't need some unhinged teenager to deal with. He ran up the dock to intercept her.

"Carrie!" Ryan yelled out, approaching her and grabbing her by both arms.

"You can't go down there. There's been a terrible accident."

Carrie craned her neck to try to peer around him while struggling to free herself.

"What do you mean, a terrible accident?"

Ryan did not answer immediately.

"Is it Mig? Tell me it's not Mig!" Carrie shrieked.

Carrie attempted to wriggle away from him, but his grip became even tighter, and then he said softly, "I'm sorry Carrie, Mig's dead."

144

Carrie's body immediately gave up the struggle; her knees buckled and collapsed as the weight of Ryan's words fell upon her like a million bricks, making her fall to the ground. She felt as if she were underwater, drifting farther out to sea, caught up in the current. It was as if someone was holding her under and she couldn't come up for air. The heavy cries and screams that were coming out of her own mouth sounded as if they belonged to someone else, someone far away. She could not lose Mig! No, this was not fair! Mig wasn't dead. He had held her in his arms just the night before. They had kissed; she had felt his heartbeat, as alive and as loud as her very own. Her heart, which just minutes ago was so full of love, so full of Mig, now felt as if it had been ripped from her ribcage by someone's bare hands. Carrie thought, *Please let Ryan be wrong.*

Nestor had been preoccupied with helping the paramedics in their attempts to revive Mig and he had not seen Carrie or all the activity on the dock. He heard the cries of a girl, glanced up, and saw that it was Carrie, curled up in a ball, with Ryan bent over her. He managed to push his way through and out of the crowd of people and rush to her side.

"Get away, Ryan. I'll take care of her," Nestor said. Not waiting for a response, he quickly nudged Ryan aside and bent down to Carrie, taking her by the shoulders and pulling her toward him. He wanted to protect her, knowing she was as fragile as fine porcelain and that this was definitely going to break her. Ryan scoffed, but actually he was all too happy to accommodate Nestor and turn over the responsibility of the distraught teen to him. Ryan needed to get back down to Mig and the other paramedics.

Tess bent down next to Nestor and wedged her way between them. She wrapped her arms around Carrie and held her close. She began to rock back and forth. "Shhh, It's okay, it's okay." Tess knew that those words were lies; why was she even saying them? She didn't know what else to do. All she knew was that Mig was hurt, or dead, if Ryan actually knew what he was talking about, and her beautiful friend was shriveling up like a wilted flower. She had only heard such heartbreaking sounds once before, when her own grandfather had died. Her Nana had made these same sounds in the hospital when the doctor had come into the waiting room to hold her hands in his and gave her the news that Papa was gone.

Gina and Donna both seemed to be in a state of shock. At a distance, they stood completely still and watched the activity down at the boat as the paramedics continued to perform CPR on Mig. *Oh my God,* Gina thought, *Mig is dead.* She looked at Donna, wide-eyed and speechless.

One of the MPs yelled out, "Clear the area! We need this dock cleared! Come on, now, everyone clear out!"

Nestor and Tess managed to get Carrie on her feet, and as instructed, they walked away from the dock.

Two paramedics placed Mig on a stretcher. Rudy, hopped up into the back of the ambulance, and along with them, carefully guided the stretcher inside. Before closing the ambulance door, one of the paramedics said to the other, "Hey, someone needs to grab his diving gear. It has to go with him."

Ryan, who was standing nearby, held up one hand and said, "No problem, I'll get it."

Rudy and the paramedic waited in the ambulance as Ryan entered the cabin of the boat to get Mig's tank. There was a long moment before Ryan came back out with the tank in hand.

"Here ya go," he said as he handed it over to Rudy.

Rudy studied Ryan for a moment and then thanked him. The paramedic closed the door.

As Ryan turned to walk away he noticed Nestor looking directly at him. He continued walking up the dock, feeling the burn of Nestor's eyes penetrating the back of his neck.

Carrie on the Rocks
TWENTY-FIVE

Even the breathtaking sunset could not upstage the loss and grief Carrie was feeling. As they walked together along the sand, Carrie told Gina and Adam that she needed some alone time and would catch up with them later. Reluctantly, they left her there to mourn her lost Mig.

She felt sick thinking of him and how he'd drowned. The ocean had been as unforgiving as her heart was broken. She sat on her favorite rock and looked out to sea, as if she expected Mig to emerge wearing his diving gear and brilliant smile, rendering this all a horrible mistake. But he did not come; only her tears came, as salty as the aqua waters that had taken him away. Over the sound of the ocean she could faintly hear Mig strumming his ukulele and singing *Tiny Bubbles,* like he had so many times before.

Feeling helpless, Adam and Gina knew that even their close friendship could not lessen Carrie's sorrow. They left Carrie on the rock alone as the waves lapped up all around her.

As they walked down the beach, Adam tossed a rock into the ocean.

"I just keep thinking about how he could have died. The thought of not being able to breathe just freaks me out. Ya know, when we were in Hono, I took a couple of scuba diving lessons at the hotel pool. It was really cool. I dug it. It's like a totally different world down there, man. I was just getting up the courage to do an ocean dive, but not now. Not after what happened to Mig and those two guys on the *Prinz Eugen.*"

Gina cocked her head quizzically. "What happened on the *Prinz Eugen?*"

Adam looked out at the ocean and sighed. "Two divers drowned checking it out. They got caught in the silt and lost their bearings. Diving wrecks can be dicey stuff, I guess."

"That's horrible," she said, shaking her head. "I'm just too claustrophobic. I could never do it."

"That was the one thing I thought I *could* do, that I would be good at. But now I don't know what I'm gonna do," he said as he threw another rock into the ocean.

Gina looked over at Adam and smiled. She knew she was looking at a good guy with a big heart. She tousled his hair and let her hand linger on his back for a moment, drawing Adam's attention.

"So," he asked, "are you and Billy still hangin' together?"

"Not really," she replied. "He's been preoccupied with all this nuke stuff."

"Do you think there's anything to it?" Adam probed.

"I don't think so. Whaddaya think? I mean, there are missiles out here. It is kinda weird." She turned back to glance at the missile range and noticed that Carrie had left the rock and was walking out to sea.

"Shit!" she shouted. Adam turned to see Carrie walking barefoot on the dangerous, serrated coral reef. The two of them bolted after her, screaming at the top of their lungs.

"Carrie, *stop! No!*" Adam sprinted past Gina after pulling his sandals from his back pocket and slipping them on.

But Carrie was numb inside and did not feel the jagged coral tearing at the bottoms of her feet. Like a magnet, she felt herself being drawn out to the deep water. The ocean turned red, swirling about her ankles and staining the beautifully transparent water around her.

Adam remembered all too well the times he had endured the painful steel-brush scrubbings from his own coral cuts. He plunged straight into the water after her, while a barefoot Gina screamed helplessly from the shore. Adam scooped Carrie up in his arms and headed back. Carrie's feet were badly bleeding; her eyes were glazed over and fixed as if she were hypnotized.

Adam eased Carrie to the ground and Gina cradled Carrie's head in her lap, stroking her hair.

"We gotcha, Care. You're okay now, sweetie." The evening siren had begun to sound.

Carrie seemed to wake from her trance and she broke down crying in Gina and Adam's arms. The three of them held each other there on the shore as the evening siren, like Carrie's uncontrollable sobs, continued to wail.

~~~~~~~

Dr. Bailer at Kwajalein Hospital tended to Carrie's wounds and by eight o'clock that night he had cleaned out and dressed the last of the lacerations on her feet. After Gina informed the doctor of her emotional state because of Mig's death, he decided that this, combined with the trauma from her injuries, justified sedation.

Adam and Gina left the hospital shortly after Carrie dozed off. The hospital staff telephoned Carrie's parents and informed them of the incident. She was quiet now but you could still see the trails from the salty tears that had spilled down her cheeks. Her bandaged feet were elevated and she lay fast asleep in the arms of Prince Valium.

The hospital halls were silent and empty and only the night nurse, Mrs. Sells, was left on duty. The sound of a door closing at the back of the hospital briefly drew the nurse's attention, but she quickly dismissed it as one of the cleaning staff.

Inside Carrie's room, a soft voice over her head said, "You're going to be all right." Her fingers moved ever so slightly. She was disoriented, and the sound of the voice tugged at her from the deep, sedated sleep she had fallen into. She struggled to open her eyes. Through two narrow slits she could see a fuzzy, dark figure bending over her. The figure was stroking her hair, and for a moment, in her stupor, a vision of Mig formed that pulled her even farther from the surface.

"Mig, is that you?" she mumbled, trying to raise her head, which seemed to weigh a thousand pounds, off the pillow.

At that moment, through the front doors of the hospital came Nestor with an injured teen that moaned and limped from a large treble hook that was lodged in his foot.

"We got trouble with treble hook." Nestor said to the nurse on duty.

"Oh, dear. There's an empty room next to Carrie's, 208. Put him down there." Nestor's look of concern made the nurse explain.

"She got some pretty severe coral cuts down at the ocean today."

"She okay?" Nestor asked as he headed down the hall with the bleeding teen.

"Yeah, she's okay, but the doctor has her sedated. I'll be down in a moment."

Nestor gave a nod and continued down the hall, reading the room numbers.

Inside Carrie's room, the silhouetted figure leaned down and began kissing her on the lips. But Carrie was slipping back as the Valium coursed through her veins. The kisses became deeper and wetter. The figure's hand moved to her face and lightly stroked her cheek. On the ring finger of the hand was a class ring with a red stone marked Nutley High School.

As Nestor passed Carrie's room with the injured teen, he glanced through the small rectangular window to her room and felt his guts wrench at what he saw: Ryan kissing the sedated Carrie!

Nestor, in knee-jerk reaction mode, released the teen and went for the door. As he reached for the door handle the teen slipped and fell, letting out a wail of pain, which momentarily derailed Nestor's rage. Nestor returned to the pained teen and quickly moved to Room 208, just as the nurse joined them with a syringe, gauze, and bandages.

A brief moment passed and Nestor emerged and ran directly back to Carrie's room but found Ryan had gone. He charged back into the hallway, only to hear the back door close. His eyes narrowed as his mind officially darted and tagged Ryan as the dangerous animal he now knew he was.

~~~~~~~

Carrie's parents arrived shortly afterward and stayed with her until she awoke late that night. When Major Conroy asked her if the accident had something to do with Mig's death, Carrie fell silent. Her parents didn't want to press her; they were just relieved to know that their daughter was safe and sound.

A Fischer in Paradise

TWENTY-SIX

As Billy made his way down the hall to his history class, he distributed a handful of anti-war flyers that he had received from Ted, to any student that would take one. By this time, the Kwajalein High student body had become accustomed to Billy's preoccupation with protesting the war in Vietnam. He pinned several up on the student activity bulletin board, making room by removing the ridiculous flyer of Martin Storm, who was running for student body president, even though everyone knew he didn't have a chance in hell of winning. Stashing the rest in his duffel bag, he made it to Bachman's class just before the bell rang.

As Mr. Bachman began to take roll, he realized Carrie's chair was empty.

"I see we're sans Carrie today. Does anybody know where she is?" Tess told him that she had some bad coral cuts on her feet but should be back soon.

Mr. Bachman furrowed his brow.

"I'm sorry to hear that. Kwaj is a beautiful place, but it can be mighty dangerous, too. I'm sure you've all heard about what happened to Mig."

A collective sigh from the students indicated the affirmative. Adam raised his hand, and Mr. Bachman acknowledged him. Adam asked, "Do you know how it happened?"

"I heard that it could've been carbon monoxide poisoning," Bachman replied as he turned to the blackboard. He could hear the murmurs from students behind him.

"It's possible someone may have messed with his air tank."

Adam said, "You mean, messed with it like accidentally, or do you mean like he was murdered?"

Bachman realized he opened a can of worms.

"I don't know. I heard that it's being investigated, so we probably shouldn't speculate at this point. Let's just see what turns up."

Gina began speaking, unsolicited.

"Wow, you mean there might be a murderer running around somewhere on the island?"

Tess spun around in her chair.

"That's crazy. Why would anyone want to hurt Mig?"

Mr. Bachman slammed on the brakes.

"Look, it doesn't do us any good to speculate. Whether Mig's death was accidental—which it more than likely was—or not, he was a great guy and will be sorely missed. Let's just leave it there for now and let's move on until we get some more information. And before we get too sidetracked, I want you to know I'm working on a field trip for you guys. We're going off-island. We'll be learning some of the history of the Marshalls, and at the same time we can address some of the questions you raised earlier in class. Just give me a little bit more time, okay?"

Billy pumped his fist in the air.

"Right on, Mr. B."

At the end of the hour the bell rang and the students began to stream out of the classroom. Mr. Bachman added, "Oh, and by the way, before I forget—I'll be here silk-screening T-shirts with Mrs. Krueger from the art department on Saturday morning, if anyone wants to join us." He turned and began erasing the blackboard.

Billy walked over to the classroom bulletin board near the door and tried to inconspicuously pin up one of the anti-war flyers. Mr. Bachman saw this in his peripheral vision and turned sharply.

"Um, Billy, you know that's not allowed."

Billy gave Mr. Bachman a pained look.

"Come on, Mr. B."

Mr. Bachman secretly liked the idea that his students were involved, that they had opinions and wanted to be heard.

"Ah, leave it. If anybody asks, I'll just tell 'em I didn't even see it, don't know where it came from."

Billy pushed the pin in hard, smiled, and turned to leave. He flashed Mr. Bachman the peace sign and walked out of the classroom with a confident bounce in his step.

~~~~~~~

Back on the mainland Ted was leading another Vietnam protest at the Berkeley campus. There were more students at this rally than any he had ever seen in the past. He was wearing his signature peace-sign armband, and he shouted into a megaphone that energized the students even more.

"This is not our war. We have to send Washington a message!" The crowd cheered wildly. As passionate as Ted was about his feelings for his country and his belief that they had no business being involved in this war, at the same time it was frightening to feel the collective energy of the students and the power they could wield. They began to move off campus now. There were thousands of them and the crowd was growing fast. This was supposed to be a peaceful protest rally, but it was more and more looking like the

Blob, swallowing up everything in its path. The patrons at a bar on University Avenue all left their barstools and went to the window, as the swarm of students oozed by, chanting, "No more war! No more war!"

Departure
TWENTY-SEVEN

Donna had spent a restless night and all of the following day waiting for Ryan to come by. He didn't show, and they had so much to talk about, so many details to go over. She wasn't ready to leave the island and definitely not this way, not without tying up all of these loose ends. My God, she was leaving tomorrow, where was he anyway?

She went into the bathroom, applied a bit of lipstick and mascara, wet her hair, and put in a few big curlers. She looked at her face in the mirror; she knew she was pretty, but when she was with Ryan, she never felt quite pretty enough. It was as though she had to work extra hard to make him notice her.

After her hair had dried, she took out the curlers, fluffed her long dark hair and hoped the humidity wouldn't straighten out the bottom flip, at least not until Ryan had a chance to see her. She slipped on a tight-fitting pink T-shirt that Ryan had commented on before, telling her that she had looked "damn sexy." That remark had left her in a good mood for days, but recently compliments from him seemed to be few and far between—he told her he didn't want her to get a big head.

She figured Ryan might be at the Yuk Club; he seemed to be spending a lot of his free time there lately and she couldn't wait another day for him to come to her. Looking at herself in the mirror one last time, she checked her teeth for traces of any leftover food, and left the house.

Ryan placed his hand on the woman's knee under the bar and teasingly ran his fingers up her inner thigh. She pulled her legs together tightly, giggled, and under her breath coyly told him to stop. She was married—to Ryan's friend, no less. They had to play it cool; everyone pretty much knew everyone on the island and made it a point to know each other's business. They had to make this look like a chance meeting here at the Yuk and that they were just sharing a friendly cocktail until her husband arrived. It was risky, but there was something about Ryan that she couldn't say no to.

Ryan looked up at the bartender.

"One more my man, and another for the lovely lady."

Donna entered the Yuk Club and rounded the corner, where she had a full view of the bar. There was Ryan. His back was to her and there was a woman sitting on the barstool next to him—and, in Donna's opinion, sitting much too close.

Who the hell is that? she thought. Even from behind, Donna could tell by her hair and the clothes she had on that the woman was older. There was no way Ryan was with her, she told herself. She felt shaky and quietly approached from behind, feeling on one hand like an intruder who had just entered someone's home uninvited, and on the other, like this woman had entered her world uninvited.

Ryan could feel the presence of someone behind him and turned sharply to see her standing there.

"Oh, hey," he said. "What's up?"

Donna cleared her throat and nervously tucked her hair behind one ear. She didn't want to talk in front of this woman, who was checking her out with great curiosity. Donna avoided eye contact with her, lowered her voice, and leaned in to Ryan.

"Can I talk to you alone? I haven't heard from you, and my flight leaves tomorrow. We need to talk."

"Yeah, sure. Absolutely," said Ryan, not wanting to rock the boat. He looked at the woman next to him and said, "Excuse me for a minute, will ya?" She nodded, turned away, and took a sip of her drink.

He swiveled around, took Donna's arm, and led her away from the bar to stand near the front door.

"Look, sorry, babe. I've been busy. And hell, I wish I could see you tonight, but I've already made plans with some of the guys."

Donna glared at Ryan, who quickly added, "But I'll come to the airport early tomorrow. We'll have plenty of time to talk then. Okay?"

That was not okay with Donna, meeting with his friends when he should be meeting with her. But she knew better than to cry or argue; he hated it when she did that. He had told her before it was a sign of weakness, and weakness in his world was not allowed. She summoned up her best Liz Taylor. *Put your best acting face on, Donna,* she told herself.

"Yeah, I guess so, Ryan. But we really have a lot of things to go over." Donna looked over at the woman.

"Who is she?"

"Her? Just a friend. She's my buddy's wife." Ryan glanced in the woman's direction. "She's nobody to me."

Donna couldn't rein in her sarcasm and jealousy.

"Your buddy's wife? Well, she's sitting awfully close to her husband's *buddy,* if you ask me."

Ryan gave her a look of disappointment.

"Wow, you don't trust me, baby. That really hurts."

Donna turned to leave.

"Hey!" Ryan yelled after her.

"You look really nice."

Donna turned to look back at him, offered him a half smile, and walked out the open door where the extreme humidity hit her as fiercely as her unpredictable feelings. She knew the timing wasn't perfect for her and Ryan, but things had happened the way they did, and it was best not to second-guess them. Seeing him today left her feeling even more confused. Along with the hormonal ping-pong game playing out inside of her and having to endure over a weeks worth of morning sickness, it was hard for Donna to deal with this racetrack of colliding thoughts and emotions.

With each and every one of their secret rendezvous, she had felt herself falling a little more in love with him. But after seeing him today, all she felt was as if she were falling apart.

~~~~~~

Donna reluctantly boarded the plane, weighed down with an overly large carry-on and a heart full of hurt. Ryan had not shown up. She had waited there for over three hours and had come up with countless excuses for him: he was called in to work, he fell and broke his leg; a dozen or so scenarios played around in her head. But that inner knowing, that jagged pit that ricocheted around in her stomach, knew better, and she futilely tried to wrestle that truth to the ground.

At least she was allowed to cry here—this was an airport, a frenzy of hellos and good-byes. It was a place where friendships were made and friendships torn apart, a place where people were uncertain they would ever meet again. They were all used to this, friends coming and going; their time was up on the island and they were off to the next destination of their parent's career move. Crying was expected, and no one had to know that the real reason she was in tears was because the man she loved, the man whose baby grew inside her, didn't care for either one of them. She already knew that the love he was withholding from them would leave a hole so large in her that she would walk around for the rest of her life partly empty.

She buckled her seat belt and looked out the small window at all of her friends who had come to see her off. She smiled as the tears fell, thinking how strange it was that she could laugh and cry at the same time. God, she loved those crazy kids. She hated leaving them. They were the best thing that had ever happened to her.

Tess waved at her sister and through the small window she could see Donna waving back. "You know, that fucker Ryan didn't even come to see her off." Tess said through clenched teeth.

Adam put his arm around her. Everyone knew that as much as Tess acted annoyed and sometimes disgusted with her sister, she loved her, and having her leave now was going to be tough. Tess couldn't help but beat herself up a bit for not being more supportive of Donna. Donna had been going through so much and Tess hadn't been there for her. And now she was leaving.

They had shared a bedroom, and many nights they would get overly tired and laugh themselves silly. Tess's mother was always yelling from the other room to quiet down, which only made them laugh harder. Tess really didn't want to sleep even one night in that bedroom alone. She missed her sister already.

Adam pulled her close but stared straight ahead.

"I had that guy pegged back at the Yuk. You know, that night he messed with that old Marshallese man? I mean, I get that Donna is hurting, but really, she's lucky. That guy's no fuckin' good. She dodged a bullet, if you ask me."

The plane began to taxi down the runway, "Bye, Donna! Love you! We'll miss you!" they all yelled out, as if singing in a round, and they waved good-bye one last time.

Jumpin' Jack Flash

TWENTY-EIGHT

It was the first time since Carrie had been released from the hospital that she felt like getting out of bed. Until today she hadn't had the energy or the desire to do anything except bury herself under the covers, refuse all offers of food, and pray she might disappear. But she caught a glimpse that morning of what might be a light at the end of the tunnel, when she woke and was craving a big bowl of corn flakes.

Joanna was very aware of what Carrie was going through; her daughter's silence and depression spoke volumes. It hadn't escaped her when Carrie seemed unusually happy or excited when she returned home from dance practice or a recital, and Joanna knew those moods had much more to do with something other than dancing.

Carrie had brought up Mig's name many times during conversations, and Joanna had noticed the feeling in her voice. But she waited for her daughter to come to her. She remembered the huge argument they'd had before they left the States, when she had said that the relationship between Carrie and a boy she liked on the mainland was "cute" and warned her it was just puppy love and not to get too serious about it. Carrie had stormed out of the room, screaming at her mother, "You don't know me! You don't know what I feel."

Joanna didn't want to make that mistake again. She wasn't going to deliver any warnings or dispense unsolicited advice unless she deemed it absolutely necessary.

She was extremely happy when Carrie came hopping out of the bedroom on one crutch and asked her mother, "Do we have any powdered milk mixed up? I really want a big bowl of cereal."

It was a glorious day; you couldn't find a better one if you traveled the globe. The trade winds were warm and gentle, the sun was partially covered by passing clouds, and the water couldn't have been any bluer.

Billy, Adam, Gina, and Tess had been waiting patiently for Carrie to come around, they didn't want to push her. Nestor had told them to give her time, telling them that she needed to heal, to process her thoughts and feelings, and advised them to just be there for her when she was ready. So they did as he told them. But on this particular morning they thought they would go by the Conroys' house, check on her, and maybe she would feel up to spending the day with them. It was too beautiful not to be outside.

Carrie was thrilled when they showed up at her door. She hadn't even realized how much she missed them. It didn't take much urging from them before she quickly changed into her clothes, brushed her teeth and hair, and hobbled outside on her crutches, her feet still bandaged.

"Wow, how is this gonna work?" she asked when it dawned on her that she couldn't ride her own bike.

"Not to worry, my fair maiden. Help me out, guys," Adam said, motioning to Billy and Gina.

They lifted Carrie onto Adam's handlebars and helped her as she shifted her weight to balance. Her feet were jutting out straight ahead, and Adam asked, "You doing okay, girl?"

Carrie smiled. "I think so. I hope I don't fall off!"

Gina and Billy each took one of Carrie's crutches and placed it across their handlebars. Adam gave the group a nod, "Okay, you guys ready? Let's go!"

As they began to ride down the middle of the street, Carrie felt nothing but pure joy. She felt secure at that moment, and happy to be back in the arms of her friends. She closed her eyes and let the wind blow back her hair.

Billy started singing in his best Mick Jagger rasp, *I was born in a crossfire hurricane, and I howled at my ma in the driving rain.*

Together Roger and Adam took up the next line: *But it's all right now, in fact it's a gas. But it's all right now, I'm Jumpin' Jack Flash, it's a gas gas gas.*

Billy tried to pass Gina, but the crutch extending from his handlebars struck a coconut tree, and he swerved, almost losing control of his bike and nearly falling to the ground.

Tess, Gina, and Carrie all started laughing hard, and for a moment it felt like old times, before Carrie's accident, before Donna had to leave, before Mig had died. Tess was more than pleased. There she was; there was Carrie, her friend, coming back to them.

The five of them on the four bikes rode past the marina where Mig's boat was moored. Adam and the others quickly realized where they were and what was happening. Carrie's face had become tight and pained. The laughter had stopped and the singing had come to a halt. An uncomfortable silence surrounded them. Adam increased his pedaling speed, as did the others, but Carrie wasn't going anywhere; her mind and heart stayed on Mig's boat and the deserted dock as they passed by.

Warhead

TWENTY-NINE

A group of men carefully moved the Zeus anti-missile warhead onto an elevator platform alongside the tall rocket on its launch pad. The rocket leaned at a forty-five-degree angle pointing over the ocean. The warhead was ready to begin its ascent. Securing the warhead was next, and required precision coordination. Ryan barked orders into a walkie-talkie.

"Secure head position and disengage."

"Warhead secure, sir," came the response he was looking for.

"Disengage when ready," Ryan said. He raised a pair of binoculars to his eyes and checked out the awaiting crew atop the gantry.

The voice over the radio replied, "Roger that. Disengaging, sir."

The platform with the Zeus anti-missile warhead on it began to move. It began a slow ascent alongside the rocket. An MP approached Ryan and handed him a note. Ryan unfolded it. It read,

Per your request to be notified, Dr. Bailer has released Carrie Conroy from the hospital, and she is now at home recovering.

Ryan thanked the MP, folded the note back up, and put it in his pocket.

A Farewell to Innocence
THIRTY

Major Conroy tapped his pipe on the edge of the ashtray until a barrel-shaped ash fell out, marking the end of the night. He folded up his tobacco pouch, put it and his pipe away in the side-table drawer, and rolled forward in the recliner he often spent his evenings in. He got to his feet, folded the newspaper under his arm and decided to finish the article on Bigfoot in the bedroom. Strolling down the hall, he knocked on Carrie's door.

"Night-night, Care," he said, expecting her reply. Nothing. He knocked again, then cracked open her door.

"Carrie, sweetie?" He cocked his head inside and flipped on the light. No sign of Carrie. A wave of concern flooded over him as he quickly moved to Roger's room.

"Rog, have you seen Carrie? She's not in her room."

Roger shook his head, and Major Conroy took off down the hall toward the kitchen, calling her name. He opened the back door and looked out into the darkness. Nothing. She was gone. Joanna came out of the bedroom, putting on her robe.

"She's not here," Major Conroy said in a voice that Joanna knew meant business.

"She's probably out with her friends," Joanna said, following her husband, who was already getting dressed and looking for a flashlight under the sink.

"If she is, she didn't say anything to me about it. Did she say anything to you?" he asked sharply. He stopped briefly, waiting for an answer.

"No, she didn't," Joanna replied, which snapped Major Conroy back into action mode.

"I'll find her. Don't worry," were his last words before the door shut and he was gone.

~~~~~~

Down at the marina, Mig's boat rocked quietly in the moonlight. Swaddled in its slip, the waves lapped at its side, creating a rhythm all its own. Carrie sat on the floor, cross-legged, in the dimly lit cabin clutching a cassette tape in her hand. Seeing her friends was great that day, but night had fallen and so had the darkness of her mood. Carrie had become well acquainted with the sadness inside her. She seemed to be accumulating painful life experiences that she had not fully owned. She reached into her bag and pulled out a tinfoil package that held two red pills. She removed them and promptly swallowed them down, then pulled her cassette recorder out of the bag and put the tape in.

She waited a long moment, knowing how difficult this was going to be, but her longing for anything Mig was compelling her. It was like passing a horrible wreck on the freeway and having to look. She had to hear his voice again, no matter how painful it might be. She pressed the play button and the audiocassette began. It was the sound of Mig doing his John Lennon impersonation:

I'd like to say thank you on behalf of the group and ourselves, and I hope we passed the audition, and that Carrie and the girls come to all the rehearsals instead of Yoko.

Carrie's emotions exploded and she quickly turned it off, realizing how powerfully the sound of his voice affected her. A sudden shift to the yaw of the boat drew Carrie's attention as Ryan came through the cabin door.

"God, you scared me. What are you doing here?" Carrie asked, as she put away the cassette player and dried off her face. Ryan slowly entered the cabin.

"I was passing by and saw a light on. I thought you might be here. I wanted to see how you're doing." He took off his jacket and sat on the captain's swivel chair.

"I'm sorry about Mig. I stopped by the hospital, but you were pretty out of it. You don't remember, do you?"

Carrie shifted on the floor uneasily.

"No, I don't remember. Why would you want to come see me anyway? You hardly even know me."

"No, but I know all about you," he said. He stood up, pulled Carrie's charm bracelet from his pocket and dangled it in front of her face. Carrie brightened, not connecting the dots.

"That's my bracelet. Where'd you get that?" She reached for it, but Ryan pulled it away. "Give it back," she demanded.

Ryan slowly returned to the chair and sat down. He turned back and said cockily, "I can't give it back. It's evidence from a crime scene."

Carrie squinted and shook her head, confused. "What? What are you talking about?"

"That's right, Carrie. I found it on Mig's bed the night I saw you at the bachelors' barracks."

Carrie suddenly realized this was serious. Ryan continued.

"You didn't know that, did you, Carrie? But I bet you did know that just entering those barracks would get you kicked off the island? Not to mention being a minor and having sex with a man nine years your senior."

"We didn't *have* sex!" Carrie protested. Then without thinking, she retaliated.

"Not like you and Donna. She told me everything," Carrie said firmly.

"Who else did she tell these crazy stories to?" Ryan asked coolly.

"Hmm, doesn't matter. Besides, who is going to believe a couple of horny high school girls over a lieutenant in the United States Army? And so you know, what I do is *not* your concern, you got that?" pointing a rigid finger in her direction.

"What should concern you is how what you've done is going to affect your parents," he added matter-of-factly.

Carrie found herself speechless at this. *How could this affect my parents?* she thought. She drew a blank, and her eyes darted about the cabin.

"I didn't do anything! Give me back my bracelet!" she said, planting both hands firmly on the floor.

Ryan casually jingled the charm bracelet again. "You can squirm all you want to, but this just doesn't look good, kiddo."

He rose and shut the cabin door and then began closing all the curtains. Her eyes followed him carefully as he did this and she began to feel her skin crawl. At the exact moment she was asking herself why he was closing the curtains in the cabin, she could feel her naiveté vanish. Her heart began pounding in her chest like a bass drum and a feeling of helplessness washed over her.

"Let me just run this down for you, Carrie, because apparently you're not too bright. Your dad will lose his job, get kicked off the island, and, to top it all off, receive a dishonorable discharge. He can kiss his career good-bye."

Carrie shook her head violently. "No!"

"Yes, Carrie!" Ryan snapped back emphatically. "And you—you will assume the title from Donna as the new island whore."

He leaned back and slowly began to applaud her. "Congratulations. Mommy and Daddy are going to be so proud of their little angel," he said with a locked smile.

Carrie's eyes began to water, this time from rage, not sadness.

"I hate you," she said flatly.

"Hey," Ryan shrugged. "No one on this island has to know except me, Carrie. The only way they're going to find out is if I tell them. And they *will* find out, believe me. But ya know, I'm in a good mood, and tonight you're in luck, 'cause I'm running a special, a two for one, so to speak. Daddy doesn't have to know, and maybe you can earn your pretty little bracelet back."

Carrie cocked her head, slowly leaned forward, and said, "What do you mean?"

Ryan unzipped his pants and waited. Carrie froze.

"Come on, Carrie, don't leave me hanging."

~~~~~~

Major Conroy saw Nestor riding by on his bike and waved him down.

"Hey, Nestor, have you seen Carrie? She's supposed to be at home."

"No, I no see her since she was in hospital," Nestor replied.

"I'm worried about her. Do you know where I might find her?"

"No worry, I will help find her." Nestor's words were a relief to Major Conroy.

When Nestor arrived at the Teen Center, it was dark. He raced to the Richardson Theater, but it was empty. Nestor knew the fourth hole was a good bet, but he cursed under his breath when he found it deserted. He was headed back to the family housing area when he passed the marina, noticed a light on in Mig's boat, and doubled back. When Nestor boarded the boat he found Carrie alone, huddled in the corner, crying. He kneeled down to her and quietly whispered, "It's okay. I'm here. I take you home."

~~~~~~~

Major Conroy opened the front door. There was Nestor, holding Carrie by the arm.

"There you are. Thank God you're all right. Where have you been?" Major Conroy asked.

Nestor explained as Carrie silently hobbled inside. "She on Mig's boat. She okay Major Conroy."

Major Conroy smiled. "Thank you, Nestor."

They shook hands as the two of them shared a look of relief. The front door closed. As Nestor turned to leave, he glanced back at Carrie's window and saw her light go off. Nestor took a deep breath, got back on his bike and headed back to the barracks.

Major Conroy peeked inside Carrie's room and saw she was already in bed, with her back to him. He wanted to talk with her but he knew it was probably more important for her to get her rest. She had been through a lot. Joanna came to his side and he motioned to Carrie there in her bed. Joanna smiled at her husband and patted him gently on the arm, and he quietly shut her door.

Carrie lay in bed with her eyes open, staring blankly into the darkness. She opened her hand, which had been gripping the charm bracelet Sara had given her. Never in a million years did Carrie ever think something so sentimental, so special, would represent something so hideous. She slowly tilted her hand and let it fall to the floor. It was now just a souvenir of her innocence.

Pink Toenails
THIRTY-ONE

It had been more than a week since Carrie had stepped foot outside the house. Losing Mig was bringing up thoughts of Sara and the helplessness she had felt back then. What had happened to her on the boat was now adding anger, bitterness, and confusion to her already fragile state of mind.

She was left empty, with no desire to see anyone, or to do anything. She had stood paralyzed in the middle of her room amidst a whirlwind of questions, yelling at God and asking him why these things had happened, but her questions remained unanswered. She didn't want to confide in her friends and definitely not in her parents, who continued to hound her with those repetitive questions: "Carrie, are you okay? You want to talk about it?"

Roger came to her room and peeked in.

"Hey, we're all meeting later at the fourth hole. You know, you might want to leave your pity party early and come join us."

Carrie glared at him and said nothing. If he only knew, she thought, maybe he wouldn't act so smug and self-righteous.

Roger, Billy, Gina, and Tess all rode up to the fourth hole on their bikes and could see that Adam had arrived ahead of them. As they walked up to greet him he let a red bandanna fall onto the green grass; opening, it revealed an ample supply of shiny silver quarters.

"Hell yeah, we've got enough quarters here to drink all night!" Adam exclaimed proudly. He began inserting quarters into the vending machine, with the Olympia Beer cans dispensing at twenty-five cents a pop. Adam handed each of them a cold one as the cans fell down the chute. Once they all had a beer in hand, they walked around to the back of the Quonset hut so as not to be seen. They sat down on the ground cross-legged and Billy passed a pack of cigarettes around.

Adam took one, lit it, and took a deep drag.

"This is the life, right, guys? I mean, really, where else would you find beer machines on the golf course?"

After pausing for just a moment, he continued, "Do you guys ever miss being on the mainland?"

Roger picked a blade of grass and began chewing on it.

"You kidding? I miss the mainland just about every day."

Adam chugged his beer and then wiped his mouth. "Yeah? What do you miss most about it?"

Billy replied, "Mainly the land."

Everyone chuckled. Billy's ego was a little pumped up, seeing how the group appreciated his pun. He went on to tell them how he missed the open fields near his old house where he used to ride his mini bike; how he missed fishing with Ted in the mountains and river rafting with his Uncle Ronny—things that a three-mile stretch of land just didn't afford you.

Roger leaned over and fetched a smoke out of Billy's pack. He spoke out of the side of his mouth as he lit it.

"Football. Real American football. I miss watching it *and* playing it. You know, soccer just isn't the same thing. I'm not really diggin' it." He blew smoke out of his nostrils.

Adam was feeling no pain; he had already finished two beers and was ready to go again. He grabbed another quarter off of the bandanna and muttered,

"Praising what is lost makes the remembrance dear."
He leaned in to Tess and with a strong English accent
said, "Billy Shakespeare, in case ya didn't know."

Tess smiled and elbowed him. It was her turn to
contribute to the *what-I-miss-most* list.

"Well, I don't know about you guys, but I miss
food—like real cow's milk, for one thing. And fast
food joints. There's nothing like McDonald's fries, or
… oh my God, did you guys ever have a Taco Bell
Burrito Supreme? Man, those are so good."

Gina agreed with her. But what she really missed
were cars, she told them. She loved driving around,
windows down, the music blasting.

"Besides cars, I miss hearing new music! Thank
God AFR plays Casey Kasem on Saturday mornings. I
just heard a new song the other day. I think it was
called "Time of the Season." It was bitchen. I loved it.
I hope he plays it again on next Saturday's show."

Just then Adam noticed Curtis as he drove by in his
cop truck.

"Curtis alert! Hit the deck!" he warned the group.
They all hit the ground face down as Curtis slowly
cruised past.

Billy whispered, "Fuckin' little prick. I spilled my
beer."

The others quietly chuckled and watched as Curtis
drove on by, and when it was safe they resumed their
upright positions. It seemed Curtis had very little crime
to attend to on the island, and so his main concern, and

self-appointed duty, was trying to bust kids either drinking or breaking curfew.

Roger thought about Carrie.

"Man, Carrie is gonna be pissed that she missed that. That is one thing that would've cracked her up."

Tess and Gina talked about how much they missed seeing her and how different the group felt when she wasn't around. Billy got up and went to the beer machine to get another. Returning, he raised his beer and said, "Well, here's to Carrie, missing in action."

No sooner had they finished toasting their beer cans together, Carrie appeared, limping her way toward them. Tess saw her first.

"Carrie, you're back! We've missed you so much!" Looking down at Carrie's bare feet, she asked, "How are you? Are your feet getting better?"

Carrie shrugged, looked down and with little emotion said, "They're getting better. I mean, look, I actually painted my toenails today."

Adam handed Carrie a cold beer and raised his.

"All right then," he said, "let's all toast to Carrie's toes."

Laughing, they all raised their beers except Carrie, who instantly became sullen and withdrawn. Adam looked at her expressionless face.

"Hey, come on, where's your sense of humor? Anyway, how ya doing, Carrie?"

Carrie didn't know what she was feeling; maybe it was too early for her to rejoin the group. She wasn't ready to go back to normal, but apparently, that is what they thought, that she was 'back' and everything was right again with the world. Well, nothing in her world was right. Her fragile emotional state snuck up and overwhelmed her.

"How the fuck do ya think I'm doing?" she snapped.

"My boyfriend just died! I just got out of the hospital! I just…" She trailed off.

"You didn't really know him long enough for him to be your boyfriend, did you?" Roger asked.

Carrie turned sharply and faced her brother. She felt nothing but hatred for him right now.

"Fuck you, Roger! I loved him, and he loved me."

Billy wanted to calm the waters and tried to intervene, but she continued, "You guys have no idea what's happened to me, or what I'm going through!"

Adam muttered beneath his breath, "Why'd ya paint your toes, then? Things can't be all *that* bad."

Carrie broke. "I painted my toenails so when I kick your fucking teeth in, my feet will look pretty doing it!"

She got up, threw her beer at Adam, and stormed off, limping her way back to her bike. Adam sat stunned and soaked, while the rest of the group was quiet, not daring to utter a word.

Billy put out his cigarette and looked at his friends. "Wow, didn't see that coming."

Tess got up and started to go after Carrie, but Gina stopped her.

"No, let's give her time. She's obviously still going through it." Tess heeded her advice and they all watched quietly as Carrie rode off.

Roger sat with his head down.

"Maybe I pushed it too far. Actually, she's going through a lot more than you all know. I think losing Mig brought up a lot of memories of our sister's death. I saw her going through all of Sara's photo albums lately. Kinda sucks."

This was the first time Carrie or Roger had ever spoken of their sister's death. It had always been the elephant in the room up until now. Adam carefully poised the question.

"What happened?

Roger looked up at Adam, then broke off a new blade of grass and put it in his mouth.

"Sara called the cops on this asshole that this other girl had invited over to our house one night when our parents were out. The way I understand it, this guy and the girl had taken some acid. The guy had punched out the girl cuz she wouldn't put out I guess—they found her passed out on the bathroom floor. Sara didn't get off so lucky. The guy caught her calling the cops and freaked."

Roger looked up and saw the others absorbing every word. Roger could feel his insides begin to tighten up.

Gina moved over and sat down next to Roger and took his hand. Roger held his breath as his emotions that had been kept under lock and key for years began to surface. His eyes brimmed with tears as he ran his fingers through his hair. It had to come out, and he knew it. It was now or never and the latter could only be worse. He squeezed Gina's hand and brought it to his chest.

"They said Sara had obviously put up quite a struggle. She was pretty beat up. He had hit Sara repeatedly with the phone receiver. They found her with the ties from one of my mom's cooking aprons wrapped around her neck floating face down in our pool. She had been beaten and strangled."

Roger paused and broke up. Gina looked up at the group helplessly. She pulled her hand from his and put it around his shoulder and pulled him in snug to her. With her other hand she lightly rubbed his other shoulder and whispered in his ear.

"It's okay, it's good to talk about it. We all love you."

Roger wiped the tears from his face, took a deep, shuddering breath, then continued.

"The girl who invited him over committed suicide just days later, so the guy was never found. Sara told Carrie to stay in our parent's bedroom that night, and not to come out. You can imagine that Carrie feels somewhat responsible for Sara's death. I was gone on a camping trip when it happened—pretty fucked up, huh?"

Roger dried his face with his t-shirt and got up. He took a deep breath and pounded the rest of his beer. The group sat stunned and silent. Adam, not quite knowing what to do, asked the only question he could think of.

"Another beer, anyone?"

A big *yes!* was the unanimous reply. Adam distributed the beer. They all sat quietly for several minutes thinking about Roger's story of Sara's death. Roger looked up at the stars that danced about. He pointed at a bright star that seemed to shimmer differently from the rest.

"That's Sara's star right there." Tess and the others looked up.

Tess began to sing softly, *Star shining bright above you, night breezes seem to whisper I love you.*

"I love that song," Adam said, and he reached for Gina's hand, pulled her up and started to slow dance. They all began singing *Dream a Little Dream of Me*, with the exception of Billy, who lit another cigarette and silently watched his best friend dance with the girl he had regretfully let go.

Nobody was sure how much time had passed, but it was evident that there had been enough time for them to establish quite a buzz. If you could be ticketed and thrown in jail for drunk driving on a bicycle, then they were all eligible for their own cell.

Their conversation that evening had gone from Carrie and Sara, to music, to Ted and the Vietnam War. Roger was getting sloppy drunk and started singing off-key: *War, what is it good for? Absolutely nothing!* Adam and Billy joined in.

They started discussing nukes, the military, and the government, and how fucked up it all was. They talked about the anti-war movement in the States and how they wished they could be part of it. As their drunken anger and spirit grew, they stumbled over to their bikes and decided to head over to the military base. They didn't really know why or what they were going to do once they got there, but it seemed like a pretty good idea at the time.

It was a miracle that they all managed to stay upright on their bikes and arrive at the base in one piece. They zigzagged their way up to the chain-link fence, their fingers clasped around the cool galvanized aluminum as they stared at the huge missile perched on the pad.

After a few minutes, Adam decided to scale the fence. And the others, thinking this might be a good idea, followed suit. But the coiled barbed-wire at the top made it impossible to get over. One by one they dropped like flies, laughing and egging each other on to try again.

Roger held an imaginary microphone to his mouth and announced in a deep broadcasting voice, "Students gathered outside the Kwajalein Missile Base, burning their draft cards and chanting, "Hell no, we won't go."

"You got that right!" Adam hollered, as he stumbled backwards. He and Tess picked up rocks from the parkway and started throwing them over the fence at the rocket, all the while chanting, "Hell no, Hell no."

Roger continued, "The students, in their angry rage, began throwing rocks at the missile."

Gina and Billy were laughing so hard they could barely stand up straight. Suddenly spotlights came on, and a siren began to sound.

"Oh, fuck!" Billy yelled.

"Let's get the hell outta here!"

They quickly stumbled over one another, got on their bikes and zoomed off, feeling empowered, like they had just contributed to the cause and had held their first, very own, anti-war rally.

Curtis Alert

THIRTY-TWO

Curtis sat in his truck on the side of a darkened street. A half-eaten pepperoni pizza sat on the backseat and he had just reached the bottom of a large bag of barbecue potato chips when the military base siren went off. His mind raced as he licked the salt from his fingers. The evening siren had already sounded hours earlier and this had to be something altogether different. He reached for the ignition, but then he realized he didn't know what to do and relaxed again. This was a military issue, no doubt. But if it weren't, he'd be all over it like white on rice. They must have picked up something on radar, he thought, or more than likely, it was just another drill.

Just then, the teens, not seeing Curtis in the shadows, raced by him, away from the military base.

Curtis's keen sense of logic and high school education quickly put two and two together, and he sprang into action. The lights and engine popped on and he raced out of the shadows after them. Billy trailed the pack; he heard the engine of the truck round the corner behind them and looked back.

"Curtis alert!" he yelled to the already fast-pedaling group.

"Let's get the fuck outta here!"

They all scattered in different directions at once. Gina took a narrow pathway between two houses. Curtis had Billy in his sights and he was gaining on him. Billy darted into an alleyway much too narrow for Curtis's truck, forcing Curtis to slam on his brakes. Billy looked back over his shoulder.

"Yesssss!" Billy beamed as he barreled down another street.

Curtis cursed to himself, then backed up and focused his chase on the others. He was soon gaining on Tess, who looked back and realized she had to act fast. She slammed on her brakes, brodied her bike 180 degrees and took off in the opposite direction. Curtis braked momentarily but then quickly continued his pursuit of Adam and Roger.

Adam glanced back over his shoulder and said, "Follow me!" He and Roger cut across a front yard, jumped their bikes over a hedge, and made a beeline for a stand of coconut trees. But Curtis was relentless; he rounded the corner and was close on their tail.

Adam pointed and yelled, "There!" and headed between two large coconut trees. By the time Curtis realized the opening between the trees was too small for his truck to fit through, it was too late. The coconut trees stopped his truck so abruptly that the half-eaten pizza on the backseat hit the windshield and stuck like glue.

"Ah, shit!" Curtis yelled, as the pizza peeled off the windshield and fell back onto the front seat.

A moment went by, then a coconut fell from the tree overhead, denting his hood.

"Fuck!" Curtis said even louder. He tried to exit his truck to continue his pursuit on foot, but his door was jammed shut by the tree.

"Fuck!" The pursuit was over. Adam and Roger looked back and began laughing so hard that they almost collided with each other. They had won, for now.

Radio Active

THIRTY-THREE

Still feeling buzzed from the fourth hole and Curtis's chase, Adam and Roger rode their bikes into the night and found themselves in Silver City at the far side of the island. Silver City was a trailer home community that had been developed in the mid-sixties. In the daytime Silver City would shine like a giant herd of neatly organized aluminum sow bugs, and at night would take on a bleak loneliness all its own.

Adam told Roger about Lenny, a guy he knew who lived in Silver City, who had a ham radio system in his trailer. Roger got excited and suggested they stop by to see if they could tune in some new music.

Lenny was unshaven when he answered the door and, from the looks of him, the expression 'trailer trash' could have been coined to describe him. He held his four-year-old son, Gregory, who was naked, and whose nose was running from both nostrils.

Lenny said to Adam, "Hey, what's up, dude?"

They exchanged greetings, and then Adam introduced him to Roger.

"We've been jonesing to hear some new music and were in the neighborhood. Wondered if we might mess with your ham radio and see if we get lucky."

"Sure thing," Lenny said. "Hey, maybe you could watch Gregory for me. I have to grab some groceries at the store."

Adam looked at the kid and put on a fake smile. Gregory didn't like the idea at all and let out a high-pitched whine.

"Sure, I guess so," Adam reluctantly agreed.

Lenny got them situated with the ham radio, threw some shorts on Gregory, and assured them he wouldn't be gone for more than an hour. Adam said, "No problem," but inside, he was saying, *Hurry the fuck up!*

Roger began switching through channels on the ham radio, while Adam rifled through Lenny's icebox looking for beer. Gregory was mad that his dad had left him and decided to become problematic. It was about nine o'clock and Adam suggested to Gregory that he go lie down and take a rest.

"No!" Gregory exclaimed. "You're not the boss of me!"

"I am until your daddy gets home. Why don't you go play with your toys then?" Adam suggested, smiling like it was a novel idea that the runny-nosed kid hadn't thought of.

"No! I don't want to!" Gregory shouted. In one quick motion he wiped the snot off his nose onto Adam's shirt and ran into the kitchen.

Roger saw this and busted up laughing. But Adam did not find it funny in the least and immediately followed Gregory into the kitchen. Roger watched and listened, wondering what Adam was going to do.

A moment later Adam backed slowly out of the kitchen with both hands up over his head. Gregory had a large butcher knife pointed at him and wore a grin from ear to ear. Roger couldn't believe his eyes.

"Gregory, what are you doing?" Adam said.

"Put down the knife."

Roger chimed in, saying, "Santa Claus isn't going to like this."

Thinking fast, Adam quickly looked around and noticed Lenny's phone. He said, "That's right, Gregory. Put down the knife, or I'm going to call Santa and tell him you've been a bad boy, and then you won't get any presents for Christmas."

But Gregory persisted, backing Adam into the living room. Adam picked up the phone receiver and showed Gregory the keypad as he dialed *S-A-N...* Gregory began to wail. Crying, he put the knife back on the kitchen counter.

Adam gave Roger a look of relief. Gregory ran into his bedroom and began playing quietly with his toys. When Adam was sure that Gregory had settled down, he joined Roger at the ham radio. Crisis averted. Now they could focus on what they had come to Lenny's for in the first place.

After about twenty minutes searching for new music, a faint voice became intelligible through the static. The voice slurred drunkenly, "Breaker, breaker, come in."

Roger hit the switch and spoke.

"Go ahead, breaker. Come on. Go ahead, breaker. Can you hear us?"

"Yes, we can hear you. Go ahead," the voice said.

Adam leaned into the mic.

"Hi, we're on Kwajalein Island. Where you located breaker?"

"We're on a fishing trawler off Kauai. Did you say you were on Kwajalein? Kwajalein Atoll? Where exactly is that?"

Adam replied, "It's about nine degrees north of the equator."

Another male voice came through the speaker. "What the hell are you doing out there?"

"The back stroke." Roger quipped. This remark cracked Adam up.

"Sorry, little joke. Actually, right now we're looking for some good music, but we go to school out here," Roger said excitedly.

"Who goes to school out there? I didn't think anything could even live out there anymore," came another burly voice.

Adam looked puzzled, "What are you talking about?"

"That place has had so much radiation that at night you can see it from space!" This was followed by laughter from the voices aboard the trawler.

"I hope you guys don't plan to have kids," another voice added.

"I don't think they'll have to worry about that, their dicks will have probably fallen off by then!" Roaring laughter on the fishing boat followed.

"Hey, fuck off, man!" barked Adam, and he switched to another channel. Adam got up, pissed off. "What the hell was that guy talking about, anyway?"

Roger just shook his head as he shut off the power to the unit.

Just then, Lenny walked in the door and Gregory came running out of his bedroom.

"Everything okay?" Lenny asked. He set down the groceries and picked up Gregory.

"Yeah, sure. Everything's just fine." Adam said sarcastically as he and Roger headed for the door.

"What happened? Where you guys going?" Lenny inquired cluelessly.

"Bowling," Roger said in a monotone.

"Bowling?" Lenny asked. "I didn't know Kwaj had a bowling alley."

~~~~~~

As Adam and Roger rode their bikes back to their neighborhood, they mulled over what the guys on the trawler had said. It was eating at them pretty bad. They passed an intersection and Roger noted, "Hey, Mr. B's house is right down there."

Adam and Roger looked at each other, got the idea at the exact same moment, and immediately swung a hard left.

Adam knocked loudly on Mr. Bachman's front door. A moment later the porch light came on, the door opened, and Mr. Bachman stood there in his boxer shorts. Adam awkwardly cleared his throat and said, "Hey, sorry to wake you, Mr. B, but can we talk to you?"

Mr. Bachman looked at his watch.

"Sure, no problem, guys. What's going on?" He motioned them in and Adam began explaining.

"Well, you know that ham radio guy, Lenny? We just came from his house and we heard some pretty crazy stuff."

Bachman interrupted him.

"Hey, hold on a minute. I'm going to go get my robe on."

Adam and Roger took seats in the dining room. They noticed a variety of black-and-white photographs displayed on the wall. Among them was a photo of Mr.

Bachman with his crewmates on the USS Allen M. Sumner, before his arm was injured.

"Whoa, check it out."

Roger pointed to another one of Bachman, with his arm around a young Marshallese woman who wore a long side braid and had a USN pendant around her neck. Roger whispered to Adam, "Check out Mr. B with the babe."

Mr. Bachman walked back into the room and sat across from the boys.

"Okay, so what happened?"

For some reason, Adam wanted to start with the Gregory story, but he quickly realized that it didn't really pertain and jumped to what the guys on the trawler had said.

"Well, we were fooling around with Lenny's ham radio, looking to hear some new music, and found some weird dudes on a fishing boat. When we told 'em where we lived, they told us that basically we're walking radioactive streetlights. This is so not cool. *Then* they told us our dicks are gonna fall off!"

Mr. Bachman laughed and leaned back in his chair.

"What? Guys, I told you, the government wouldn't let us live out here if it wasn't safe."

He paused, but Adam and Roger just sat there. Bachman continued.

"I wouldn't pay any attention to those jerks. Remember, anybody can be out there using a ham radio. Sounds like they were just trying to have a little fun with you."

This made a bit more sense to Adam.

"Yeah, I guess you're right Mr. B, I feel like a jerk."

Roger added, "Yeah, me too. Sorry, Mr. B."

"No problem," Mr. Bachman said, getting up.

"It's kind of late. Why don't you guys go get some sleep, okay? Hey, am I going to see you tomorrow morning?"

"Yeah," Roger said as he got to his feet.

"We'll be there."

"Great. Okay, see you guys then." Mr. Bachman opened the door and gave them each a pat on the back.

"Oh, and be careful, it's past curfew, you guys don't want to run in to Curtis," Bachman reminded them.

Adam turned to Roger, and under his breath said, "We already did."

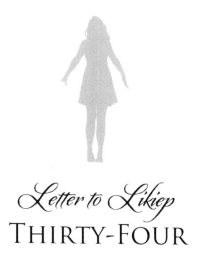

Letter to Likiep
THIRTY-FOUR

Roger and Adam still felt a bit rattled from the encounter with the fisherman on the ham radio the night before, even after Mr. Bachman's reassurance that they had nothing to worry about. But it still wasn't that easy to shake.

They met up in the morning, just the two of them, and talked briefly about their wild night. They shared their fear about the possibility of losing their dicks, which they now seemed to be checking on a minute-by-minute basis.

Adam still couldn't get over how little Gregory had almost taken him out with a kitchen knife. They both had a good belly laugh over it and couldn't wait to tell the others.

When they arrived at school on Saturday morning and rounded the blacktop toward Mr. Bachman's classroom, they could see Gina, Tess, and to their surprise, Carrie. They were getting situated at one of the long folding tables beneath the large peace sign flag that waved proudly outside Bachman's door. The girls were assisting Mrs. Krueger, the art teacher, by laying out drop cloths, squeegees, and screened wooden frames around the table. Billy lifted a box of cheap gray T-shirts, peace sign stencils, and what felt like a boatload of white paint onto the table as Mrs. Krueger instructed.

Mr. Bachman was busy adjusting the small portable radio that he had placed outside on a desk chair. Casey Kasem's Saturday morning Top 20 countdown was playing loudly, and lately it seemed to be dominated by anti-war songs. Richie Havens' soulful and spiritual song *Freedom* blasted through the tiny scratchy speakers.

"Hey!"

Adam and Roger shouted to the group as they walked up.

Mr. Bachman turned to see the boys and smiled.

"Good morning, you two. Sleep okay last night?" He walked over and patted Adam on the back.

Adam shrugged.

"Yeah, sorry about last night, Mr. B. Felt kinda stupid after we left your house."

Bachman hit him a little harder on the shoulder.

"Don't even think about it. You had some good questions, and I would've done the same thing. But like I told you guys, I think you were more than likely talking to a group of drunk fishermen who were just messing with you, that's all."

Adam snickered, somewhat embarrassed, and then went over to settle in at the table with his friends.

Just then, Mrs. Krueger shouted out to everyone to get seated, as she was ready to begin and wanted everyone's attention.

Tess looked at Roger and Adam.

"Glad you guys managed to show up. And by the way, you both look like hell. Rough night?"

Roger ignored her. Adam raised his eyebrows and responded, "You kiddin' me? You don't know the half of it." He nudged Billy and said, "We'll tell you all about it when Mrs. K stops babbling. But dude, it was insane."

"Looking forward to it, and I hope you have some Polaroids." Billy laughed as he arranged all of his necessary art supplies in front of him.

Carrie was quiet. She seemed engrossed in her project as she followed Mrs. Krueger's instructions carefully. She could faintly hear the conversations going on around her and hear the music, but to her it still felt like all the activity was off in the distance, that she was on the outside, looking in. She wasn't at home yet, not with herself, and definitely not with her classmates. The others noticed, but they were just happy to have her there, so they let her be and didn't push her with questions or demand she partake in their lighthearted conversations.

Mr. Bachman began walking around each table, checking on their progress, helping out when necessary, and in general providing words of encouragement.

When he came up behind Carrie, he placed his hand softly on her shoulder. Cautiously he said, "Good to have you back, Carrie."

She looked up at him, smiled slightly, but said nothing. He felt he needed to say more.

"And I want you to know, I'm so sorry about Mig. I know how hard this must be for you."

He hesitated for a moment and then leaned in closer, asking her discreetly and with sincere concern, "Are you doing okay?"

Carrie looked up at Mr. Bachman, but it was like she was looking right through him.

"I guess so," was her unconvincing reply. He squeezed her shoulder gently. Knowing when to let things be, he walked on to the next table.

About thirty minutes had passed and Gina was getting frustrated with the mess, wiping the white paint from her hands onto the wet rags that were placed randomly at each table.

"Ugh," she let out in irritation.

"Where is Bachman? I need some help!"

She turned around, searching for him, and caught a glimpse of him walking back into his classroom. Mrs. Krueger was busy at the next table, helping several other students, and it looked like she wasn't going to be free anytime soon. Gina figured she would wait out her misery until Mr. Bachman could come back and assist her.

Bachman let out a big sigh and sat down at his desk. He put his fist under his chin, looking like Rodin's *The Thinker,* and then pulled some stationery out of his desk drawer. He continued to contemplate long and hard about what he was going to write. His memories seemed to transport him to a place where he hesitated to travel, but he knew it to be a necessary destination. When he was ready, he began writing in a deliberate fashion.

He finished and folded the letter up slowly. He placed it in an envelope, licked it to seal and grimaced at the glue taste on his tongue. The outbound letter was ready to be sent and would soon be on the next boat out, heading off to the island of Likiep.

American Graffiti
THIRTY-FIVE

The beer and conversation flowed at the fourth hole that Saturday afternoon as Billy, Adam, Gina, Roger, and Tess, once again, passed some time without their pal Carrie. Tess and Gina were wearing the new peace sign T-shirts they had just made. Gina was modeling hers for the boys, taking the opportunity to show off, posing sexily.

Tess grabbed Gina by the leg and pulled her back to the grass.

"Earth to Gina. Sorry, boys, the fourth hole runway show is over."

"Ahhhh." Adam scrunched his face at Tess. She smirked in his direction and then brought the attention back to her own shirt.

"That was really fun today. I think these shirts turned out great."

She looked over at Roger.

"I was so surprised Carrie showed up. I wasn't expecting that."

Roger just shrugged, as if he couldn't predict what his sister was all about and what she might do these days.

Billy hadn't been paying much attention to the conversation and seemed preoccupied with his own thoughts. He brightened and then leaned forward, pulling a letter out of his back pocket and began opening it up.

"Oh wow, I almost forgot. I got a letter from Ted today!"

From the envelope, he pulled out a postcard that read, *War is not healthy for children and other living things.*

Billy flipped it over and showed them.

"Pretty cool, huh?"

He felt something else inside the envelope and examined the contents more closely.

"Cool, look what else he sent me." Billy held up a joint.

Adam smiled and snagged it out of his hand, saying, "You mean sent *us*, dude."

Adam immediately looked around, found a match, and sparked it up. Billy began reading the back of the postcard as they passed the doobie.

"This is so messed up. My brother's getting issued a lottery number next week. Fuck!"

He closed his eyes momentarily and then looked up at the group.

"He might hafta go fight a war we shouldn't even be fighting, man."

There was a silent moment before Adam spoke.

"Well, it's not like he didn't make himself a target with all that protesting and shit."

Billy shook his head at Adam in disgust.

"That's what you think? Protesting has nothing to do with that, paramecium-brain! At least he's standing up for something important, something he believes in."

Billy let fly a zinger.

"And besides, Adam, seems like the most important thing you believe in is that you shouldn't have to pay for the extra weight *seeds* add to an ounce of pot."

This earned a laugh from Gina and Tess. Adam didn't recognize the slam and said, "Well, you shouldn't." A low sigh seeped from several of the others.

Adam looked around and shrugged. "What?"

Billy sat quietly and just studied the postcard from Ted.

That evening Billy sat alone at the Teen Center writing Ted back as the Buffalo Springfield song *For What It's Worth* played on the sound system. Billy stopped at the lyric, *It starts when you're always afraid. You step out of line, the man come and take you away.*

~~~~~~

Later that week on the mainland, Ted was reading the letter from Billy at the Steppenwolf Pub. Images played on the TV over the bar: shots of young soldiers in line waiting for haircuts, shots of hair falling on the floor, shots of jarheads getting their greens, and shots of them training at boot camp.

Many of Ted's friends who also were getting issued lottery numbers that night began to congregate in the pub. If you got a high number, say between 300 and 365, you were safe. The reality of what was happening became more and more evident as the pub filled with somber young men from Berkeley and the surrounding area. The random drawing that would determine the lives of so many was about to be broadcast. It was time, and all eyes were on the TV. Ted held back the emotional and physical feelings that shot through his body as the numbers were read. He made it through the first hundred numbers but still couldn't find relief in his thoughts. After about two-thirds of the numbers had been drawn, Ted walked out. He really didn't care anymore.

The next morning Ted and Jennifer read it in the local newspaper. There were three columns, and he found his birthday, October 1, along with his number, 59, in the last column.

~~~~~~~

It was 5 a.m. and the Kwajalein sky was turning a spectacular ultramarine blue and was completely void of clouds. A C-141 Starlifter cargo carrier reduced its speed and altitude on its approach to the runway. In the cockpit a compressed voice chirped over the radio.

"Go 41 Bravo. You're clear for approach."

"Copy that," replied the pilot as he tilted his head for a visual on the runway. He noticed something odd: a very large white peace sign had been painted on it. The pilot shook his head and said, "Oh, brother. Commander's not gonna like that."

~~~~~~~

Four hours later Mr. Bachman was passing out assignments. He talked as he walked down each row.

"For those of you interested, make sure you pass in your signed permission slips for this Saturday's field trip."

Just then the door swung open and the doorway was filled with the presence of the Commanding General. A hush fell over the students. He slowly entered the classroom, followed by his son, Lieutenant Ryan Mitchell. The General stood there for a long moment, while Ryan stood at attention by his side. The General eyeballed the students warily. He began to walk slowly between the desks.

"One of you, I'm told, has taken the liberty of creating a work of art on my runway. Well, I don't like art, and I definitely don't like hippies. When I find the individual who took it upon him or herself to ignore trespassing signs and to violate military property, not to mention the vandalism committed, I will personally see to it that this individual is issued a one-way ticket off this rock and never comes back again. Do I make myself clear?"

It was so quiet in the classroom that you could hear a mouse sneeze in a bale of cotton. The General made his way back to the front of the class. He turned to leave but stopped short and doubled back. General Mitchell's eyes narrowed as he shot Ryan a look; it was a look Ryan knew all too well from the many hunting trips spent with his father, in those intense moments when his dad had spied a buck move in the dense woods a hundred feet away. The anvil of

General Mitchell's unholy wrath was about to drop, and somebody's day was about to be ruined.

The General took off his hat and slowly headed back into the classroom. His patent leather shoes squeaked as they led him over to the window, where he stood looking out with his back to Adam's desk. Adam nervously scratched his ear, revealing white paint on his forearm. Billy's eyes bugged out as he and several other students saw this. Billy looked to see if Ryan Mitchell had also noticed but found he was busy admiring Gina's legs. Mr. Bachman was staring at the floor, holding the assignments, fuming inside at the intrusion. Billy nudged Adam, motioning to the paint on his arm. Adam saw the paint and quickly hid his arm under his desk, trying to act casual.

The General pulled out a cigarette, tapped the filter on his lighter, lit it, and blew a long trail of smoke against the glass. The smoke billowed backward, encircling his high and tight haircut.

"Good view you have here, Mr. Bachman—practically a front-row seat of the radar transmitter golf ball."

He turned to look at Mr. Bachman, chuckled to himself, and replaced his hat. The General tapped his thumb on the window.

"Altair: The most powerful radar system in the world. Can track an object the size of a kitchen sink at twenty thousand miles."

"Is that so?" Mr. Bachman replied, feigning interest.

The General threw his cigarette on the floor and stamped it out while simultaneously turning and grabbing Adam's arm, holding it up to reveal the white paint. The General looked up, smiled at Bachman, and said, "There's nothing like good radar."

The General's gaze shifted to Ryan.

"Lieutenant Mitchell, a hand please with this youngster."

Ryan, following orders, quickly moved to Adam, clenched the back of his neck, and escorted him out of the room. The General followed. It was all Mr. Bachman could do to remain silent as he watched Adam being led away. The General had bagged his buck.

The next day after school, Mr. Bachman paid the Kwajalein police station a visit. He had hoped that by now things would have cooled off a bit and the General would listen to reason. He hurried up the steps, entered the station, and approached the MP on duty.

"Can you contact the General for me? It's about one of my students he arrested yesterday."

The MP gave Bachman a direct look, through his eyebrows, that didn't exactly scream friendly. He picked up the phone, dialed a number, and said, "Excuse me, I have Mr. Bachman here to speak with General Mitchell."

The MP handed the telephone to Bachman.

"I'm sorry to bother you, sir, but I need to speak with you about one of my students, Adam Wilson…"

By the time the conversation was over, Mr. Bachman had managed to convince the General that if he didn't have some concrete evidence against Adam, he would have to arrest his entire class, as they were all using the white paint while silk-screening T-shirts that past Saturday.

The idea of arresting all of the students actually appealed to the General for a moment, until he realized the ramifications. These were the kids of many of his officers, and things could possibly get sticky. He quickly dismissed the notion and reluctantly acquiesced. Adam was free to go.

Thirty minutes later Adam and Mr. Bachman walked down the front steps of the police station. Adam thanked Mr. B and asked how he had done it. Bachman just told him that he'd always had a way with his commanding officers when he was enlisted. Adam already respected Mr. B, but this move put him on a whole new level.

Adam saw Gina waiting out front for him and smiled. Mr. Bachman smiled, too, gave him a pat on the back, and headed off.

"See you at the marina for the field trip, Adam."

"Sure thing, Mr. B, I'll be there. Thanks!"

Adam watched him go. When Gina greeted him, Adam wrapped his arms around her and gave her a kiss.

"Thanks for coming. I can't believe Bachman got me off the hook, and he didn't even ask me who did it." Then Adam realized something.

"You know, I don't think he even wants to know." He looked at Gina, kind of blown away.

"Pretty cool, huh?"

Gina clasped his hand in hers and they began walking. She looked back over her shoulder at Mr. Bachman and said, "He's one of us. He always has been."

The Field Trip
THIRTY-SIX

The sun had not yet risen, and Mr. Bachman sat at his dining room table having his morning coffee and a cigarette. He hadn't slept well, knowing this day was ahead. As he studied the framed photographs on his wall, he knew this field trip to Likiep was going far beyond the scope of his teaching responsibilities and could even be construed as sedition by some.

But for Mr. Bachman there was something much deeper going on than a group of students who were thirsting for knowledge. The actions of the past had followed them into the present, and the onus was on him to do the right thing, even though the price of knowledge could drop on them all like a bomb.

~~~~~~

It was 6 a.m. at the marina and the tropical sunrise was breathtaking and beautifully fitting to offset the tone of the day's upcoming revelations. Mr. Bachman handed out life jackets and started up the Boston Whaler. Carrie, Adam, Tess, Billy, Roger, and Gina found seats and Bachman walked the boat backward out of the slip. Somehow he'd known that only these six would show up and sacrifice their Saturday. He knew they were growing up, which was unusual among the many immature high school kids he taught. It was his responsibility to encourage their struggle for knowledge; after all, this was why he'd become a history teacher in the first place.

Shifting into drive, the Boston Whaler motored slowly out of the marina, found open water, and throttled up into the blue beyond. Within ten minutes they were but a speck on the horizon.

It quickly became pointless for Carrie to try to keep her hair from becoming a complete bird's nest, and she finally gave up, letting the wind have its way. Billy was the first to break the silence. He had to speak loudly enough to be heard over the sound of the motor.

"So, what's this trip all about, Mr. B?"

Bachman turned to Billy and smiled. "We're going to get you guys some answers today."

"About Vietnam?" Billy asked.

"No, Vietnam can wait for a classroom discussion. Our topic today is the history behind these islands," Bachman said, motioning to the distant atolls.

Billy asked, "We're going to Bikini Island, aren't we, Mr. B?"

Mr. Bachman shook his head.

"Nope. That island will be off-limits for many years, Billy. In fact, some say for as many as thirty thousand years."

When the kids shared looks of surprise with one another, Mr. Bachman realized that the day's lesson had already begun. He figured there was no time like the present to pull the Band-Aid off fast and get to the meat of it. So he continued.

"In 1946, the United States started detonating atomic bombs on a regular basis out here. They tested over sixty-five nuclear bombs here in the Marshall Islands. They told the Marshallese natives on Bikini that they wanted to use their island for nuclear bomb testing, to end all war in the name of God."

Bachman noticed this got a reaction from all of them.

"Yeah, I know," he said almost guiltily.

"The most powerful blast of all was called Castle Bravo, detonated on Bikini Island on March 1, 1954. It was a fifteen-megaton hydrogen bomb, the largest bomb ever detonated in the history of the United States. Just to give you an idea, it was a thousand times more powerful than the bomb we dropped on Hiroshima."

Adam gasped.

"Holy shit!"

Mr. Bachman looked at Adam and said, "Yeah, you could say that. And interestingly enough, that is where those bikinis you girls wear, got their name. The French designer of that suit named it that for a couple of reasons. One, the entire middle was gone, blown away, just like the island, and also he thought it would cause an explosive reaction around the world."

He continued, "But anyway, the wind shifted, and several nearby islands got the fallout. The natives weren't evacuated for days. According to the military, Kwaj and the other islands were not affected, but there are some who say differently. I don't know, but what I do know is that what you're going to learn today, you won't find in any history books."

Gina slid closer to Adam, took his arm, and under her breath said, "Whoa."

A long moment passed before Billy asked, "Then... where are we going?"

Mr. Bachman looked out at a dot on the horizon, motioned with his head, and said, "Likiep."

As the Boston Whaler approached the marina on Likiep, Mr. Bachman waved, and several Marshallese men on the dock waved back. It was obvious from the smiles on their faces that they knew each other. As they got closer, Mr. Bachman spoke a few words in Marshallese to them, which surprised the students. One of the old men helped tie up the boat, and another helped them get off the Whaler and onto the dock. They left their life jackets in the boat and followed the old man onto the shore. He led them to a primitive village surrounded by grass huts and makeshift shelters.

Nearby, a group of Marshallese children happily played stickball. Their ragged clothes and dirty faces read poverty, but it was obvious from the fun they were having that they were not at all aware of it.

The students and Mr. Bachman were led under the shade of several large coconut trees where some blankets were spread out on the ground awaiting them. Several tattered lawn chairs were also set up, and the smoke from a smoldering fire pit wafted up into the tall trees. The young children noticed the students, curtailed their play, and curiously approached them. A Marshallese girl who was about ten years old approached Carrie, extending the hollowed-out coconut shell that they were using as a ball, and spoke in Marshallese.

"Iakiu?" she said softly. Carrie shrugged her shoulders and looked to Mr. Bachman for help.

"I think they want you to join them in a game." Bachman said.

Tess asked, "What game?"

"Just think baseball, and you'll be fine," Bachman explained as he motioned for them to go.

"I'll call you over when we're ready for you."

The students joined the kids and began to play. The language barrier was no problem. Mr. Bachman marveled how a simple game of stickball could join two cultures that were so very different. Adam was up to bat, and the group automatically began to back up, realizing his size and build. The coconut was pitched, and Adam smacked it high up into the coconut trees. The coconut hit another group of coconuts, which dislodged them and sent them all falling to the ground. The Marshallese girl who went to retrieve the ball couldn't tell which coconut was the ball. This drew big laughs from all of the kids and everyone around. To Mr. Bachman, this moment was worth the whole trip. He clapped his hands and laughed out loud. He couldn't have removed the smile from his face if he'd wanted to.

One of the Marshallese children hit the ball hard, a grounder, and Carrie ran after it. She followed it around to the side of a small hut and bent down to retrieve it. When she raised her head, she saw a Marshallese woman, very pregnant, sitting on a stump. A Marshallese man stood next to her, rubbing her back. They both looked very serious. Carrie studied them for a moment and said, "Oh, sorry, didn't mean to intrude. I'm Carrie." She pointed toward the others. "I'm with Mr. Bachman's class."

The pregnant woman said, "Is okay. I am Kita. My husband, Kino."

Carrie smiled and gave them a wave before she ran back to the children with the ball in hand.

Twenty minutes later an old Marshallese woman emerged from a hut with an older man by her side. Mr. Bachman noticed this and walked over, greeting them with hugs. He looked over to his students playing stickball and yelled, "Hey, guys, we're ready for you!"

The students thanked the kids for the game and gave them a wave. Carrie was wearing a peace sign necklace. She noticed the girl who had first approached them looking at it. Carrie took it off and placed it around the young girl's neck. The girl glowed and smiled brightly at Carrie, saying, *"Kommol,"* which Carrie figured was 'Thank you' in Marshallese. She smiled back, waved, and headed back with the others to Mr. Bachman.

The students all sat on the blankets and got comfortable. Adam and Roger recognized the old Marshallese woman from the photographs they had seen at Bachman's house. Mr. Bachman introduced the old woman with the crinkly, kind face as Miaka.

Miaka still wore the long side braid and had the USN pendant around her neck on a strap of thin leather. She looked around at all the young faces, smiled at Mr. Bachman, and sat down in the rickety lawn chair. The old Marshallese man moved over to her and stood behind her with his hands on her shoulders. Miaka reached up as if for support and held his hands tightly. She then placed her hands in her lap, leaned forward, and began to speak to the students.

"I was born May 4, 1937. I am from Rongelap. I was seventeen and pregnant in 1954. The sun seemed like it was shining from everywhere that morning. We hear a loud thunder. On that warm, sunny day my brothers and sisters did not know what was falling from the sky. It was like snow."

Carrie looked over at the children still playing stickball and began to imagine what the woman was describing.

Miaka continued.

"They played in it laughing, reaching up at the flakes as it covered the island in all white. We did not know it was bomb. We are simple people. We had no understanding of bomb. We were thankful to America for free us from Japanese and help us. When America ask us to help them, we are so grateful. We want to help, we trust America. After two days the ground was white with ash. They take us from Rongelap. I lost my baby to miscarriage. Three years after bomb they return us home, they tell us it is now clean and safe. But it was not."

Miaka looked away as her eyes filled with water. The old Marshallese man began to stroke her hair. She took a deep breath and continued.

"I notice that not everything was right. The arrowroot that before grew everywhere was gone. The coconut tree grow green and yellow nut—very unusual. The water change color when we cook our food. Our fish had problem. We cut open, put in water, the water change to color of rainbow.

At first they tell us not to eat the coconut crab, which were many on Rongelap, but later said it fine to eat them. During these times there is shortage of food. We develop blister all over our mouth, but we continue to eat because we so hungry."

Gina's emotions welled, her nostrils flared, and she was about to cry. She pressed her hand to her chest and held her breath as Miaka went on.

"We keep eating food from crop that grow in bad soil. I become very sick with convulsion. I cannot be in daylight long. All windows and doors of house we keep shut."

Roger looked at the hut Miaka had emerged from. All the windows were covered with tin foil.

"I have seven children, and some not right. I have many lost baby. One time, the child I miscarry was badly deform. It only have one eye. Our culture and religion teach us that deform baby is sign that wife unfaithful to husband. For this reason, many mother keep quiet about deform birth. They give birth in private, but not to baby we think of, to things like monster or jellyfish baby. We do not have Marshallese word for this kind baby, because they were never born before radiation come. Many women on Rongelap, Likiep, Ailuk, and other island in the Marshalls have all give birth to this kind baby. One woman on island give birth to baby with two head."

Carrie held her hands to her face in horror, visualizing what Miaka was describing.

"Her cat also give birth to kitten with two head. There is young girl on Ailuk today with no knees, three toes on each foot, and missing arm. Many baby born with no bones in body and with transparent skin. We see their brain and heart beating, but they die soon, and we quickly dig hole and bury. Many mother die too."

Miaka stopped and looked at the students and Mr. Bachman. From the look on all of their faces she knew it was time to draw it to a close.

"Yes, we agree to test big bomb, but we no understand what it was. We help in name of God, but we must have different God."

The old Marshallese man helped her to her feet.

"I must go inside now, sun too bright. May God be kind to you and your children," she said.

She bowed graciously to the students and then to Mr. Bachman. Mr. Bachman bowed back, then thanked her as they hugged. She turned and disappeared with the old man back into the hut, and it was over.

Mr. Bachman turned around, and all the students were on their feet. It was an act of respect. This caught Mr. Bachman off guard. He quickly turned away and wiped the tears from his eyes. He was so moved and proud of all of them. They followed him silently through the village and back to the awaiting Boston Whaler.

They all sat apart from each other on the way back. The drone of the engine wasn't loud enough to drown out what they had just learned. Locked in a reflective silence, they all felt as one, and a common understanding seemed to permeate the group. A thick blanket of dark clouds moved in and blocked out the sun, followed by a warm rain that seemed to create an emotional camouflage. For the passengers of the tiny Boston Whaler, their field trip had come to an end, but their education about the reality of the world had just begun.

The Other Side of the Coin
THIRTY-SEVEN

Carrie's head was about to explode, stuffed full of images from Miaka's unthinkable story. She tried to steer her mind away from all of the horrific imagery, but it overpowered her and took her back. Like a newsreel, scene after scene played out in her head.

She curled up on her bed. Though it was hot and muggy outside, she felt such a spine-chilling cold within her, she swaddled herself up in a blanket. She felt sickened and exhausted from the field trip. There had been so much to take in.

She grabbed a *Teen* magazine off of her nightstand, and flipped it open. It didn't matter to which page; she just needed to fill her head with gossip or fashion—something totally mindless.

Magoo seemed to appear out of nowhere, leaping up on her bed and speaking to her with his loud, needy meows.

Without looking up, she began to pet him on the head. He leaned up against her magazine, pressing his comforting weight toward her while his tail bobbed up and over the top of her reading material. Carrie tried to ignore him, but his meows became more persistent, demanding her attention. She smiled to herself and lowered the magazine, finally giving in to him.

"Magoo, what do you want?"

He jumped off the bed and ran down the hallway, as if he wanted to show her something.

Suddenly Carrie could hear the faint cries of a baby. *A baby?* Then it crossed her mind that it must be the neighbor's baby girl, Vanessa, whom her mother, Joanna, looked after from time to time. Carrie investigated, moving slowly down the hallway, as the cries grew louder.

When she reached the room where the sounds were coming from, the door was ajar, and Carrie slowly pushed it open. The room was cloaked in a neon blue light, and there in the corner was a portable crib. A slight mist enhanced a beam of moonlight that streamed in through the open window. A chilled breeze blew sheer curtains that wafted up and over the crib. Carrie quickly moved to the window and closed it. So many questions raced through her mind. She approached the crib with apprehension, quietly, so as not to disturb the baby. She peered down into the bed, her eyes widening in horror at the transparent, jellyfish-like baby, with wet, marbled eyes that undulated in a slimy film. Carrie raised her hands to her face, and backing up, let out a blood-curdling scream.

She awoke from this nightmare in a cold sweat, entangled in the blanket that she had wrapped herself in, struggling to get free. She jumped to her feet with her hand to her chest, gasping for air. She backed up into her bookshelf, knocking the *Tonna* shell that Mig had given her onto the floor. In an emotional breakdown, and in complete and utter resignation, she picked up the shell and threw it, shattering her bedroom window.

"Oh, fuck!" she cried in despair. She turned, and ran out of her bedroom and out onto the front porch. Realizing she had nowhere to go, she sat down, pulled her knees to her chest, wrapped her arms around them, and began to rock, wanting to dissolve into a little ball—one that she hoped would roll away and never come back.

"What the hell was that?" Major Conroy asked Joanna, as he reached over and turned on the table lamp next to his bed. "Stay here," he told her, and he hurried out of their bedroom to investigate.

Walking past Carrie's room, he immediately saw the shattered glass on the floor. He found Carrie on the front porch. She looked small and helpless, and was curled up in a position familiar to him, as it was one that he had seen many times before when she was little and afraid.

He didn't want to startle her by coming up behind her, so he spoke loudly.

"Carrie, honey, are you okay? What happened?"

Her first thought was that she was in trouble for breaking the window. Without looking up, she apologized, "I'm sorry, Daddy. I didn't mean to break the window. I had a horrible nightmare, and it scared me so bad."

Major Conroy sat down next to her and placed his hand on her knee.

"What was the nightmare about?"

Carrie didn't know where to start. It felt good just having her dad next to her; he seemed to be one of the few things left in her world that she could depend on. She always felt so safe whenever he was near, like nothing and no one could hurt her. She leaned into him.

"Why in the world would anyone drop a bomb that would hurt so many people?" She looked up into her father's eyes.

Major Conroy wrapped his arm around her and held her close. He looked off into the distance and took his time responding, because, truthfully, he didn't really have the answer for that. It baffled him too. But he needed to help her understand, to see things from different perspectives.

He began slowly.

"Sweetheart, let me say this. There really is nothing easy or black-and-white about this topic. If there were simple answers to this stuff, war, for one thing, wouldn't be so controversial."

Joanna had come out to the living room and peered out the front window. She saw them both sitting and wanted to join her husband and Carrie on the porch, but then she thought twice about it. It looked like an intimate moment, and she knew that whatever had just happened with Carrie, there was nobody that could comfort her better than her father. She stood still and could faintly hear his words to Carrie through the closed door.

As Major Conroy spoke in his deep, soothing voice, Carrie listened to both her father's words and his heartbeat. She wanted him to rescue her from this confused world she had found herself living in.

Major Conroy continued.

"I know it's crazy to even try and justify things like the atom bomb, honey. But on the other hand, if we hadn't used it, World War II might have continued on for God only knows how many more years. And who knows how many more people might have died."

Carrie looked up at her father.

"So are you saying that you actually think it was okay?"

Major Conroy shook his head slowly.

"No, I'm not saying it was okay. But what I am saying is that without the world being open to new ideas, or trying new things, good or bad, there would be no progress. It's how we learn, and most often we learn from our mistakes."

Major Conroy took a deep breath.

"People have to take risks. For example, if someone hadn't experimented with mold, they would never have discovered penicillin, and people would still be dying from simple infections today. I know that might seem like a minor example, but I think you get the idea."

He thought for a moment.

"Look, there *is* something irreversible about acquiring knowledge—I understand that. But if we allow ourselves to become hardened by the things the world does, or hardened by the things that happen to us, then we become afraid to live our lives. Losing Sara could have easily destroyed this family, but we're making it. I'm sure Mig's death seems senseless, too. But if we just check out, we become spectators in life instead of participants, you know. We can't let that happen—that's no way to live. *You* can't let that happen, Care."

Carrie pondered his words. She wasn't sure what she was feeling, other than pure love for her father.

"I love you, Dad."

In Gods' Hands

THIRTY-EIGHT

With the early morning sun burning his eyes, Kino ran like a gazelle. His feet seemed to float atop the rocks and coral as he raced back to the hut, carrying a basin of hot water. He miraculously maintained his balance so as not to spill a drop of this precious commodity.

When he pushed aside the grass covering that shielded the doorway, Miaka was sitting at Kita's bedside, where she lay in excruciating pain and with a blistering fever that wouldn't break. Kino was relieved to find Miaka there, knowing that she had been through this many times before and had been like a midwife to many of the women on Likiep. He himself had felt quite helpless and knew that there was nothing that a daughter needed more than a mother at her side during these difficult times.

Miaka stood when she saw Kino enter and motioned for him to take her place by Kita's side. He carefully placed the water basin near the foot of the bed, and Miaka handed him a dry cloth. He gently dabbed Kita's forehead and wiped the sweat from around her neck, then dipped the cloth in the hot water. He quickly wrung out the excess and laid it on her forehead as she grimaced and cradled her stomach in pain.

Miaka went to the corner of the hut and began preparing a mixture of broken coconut shells, fronds, shards of pig bone, and seeds to burn. It was an offering to the Gods, used to ward off any evil spirits and to bring good luck. She dug a hole in the dirt, filled it with the concoction, lit it, and let it burn. She tended to the fire, humming a lullaby that she had sung to Kita every morning when she was a child. It had always calmed her. The last thing Miaka wanted to convey was any fear, although she had plenty. She was afraid that Kita might not survive, and if she did, she feared what horrors might await her.

As she stared into the flames, Miaka thought back to the many babies she had seen born over the years: the ones with feet like clubs; the jellyfish babies with no spines, head or arms; the ones that would last only a couple of hours, and she and the other matriarchs would quickly remove them from the birth mother's sight, for fear it might make her go crazy.

Yes, she remembered. She remembered her own, and she prayed to her God, harder than she had ever prayed before, to spare Kita's life and to bring her a whole grandchild.

She stirred the fire and was lost momentarily in the dance of the flames until she was startled when Kita let out a sudden cry. Kino removed a towel that had been placed between Kita's thighs, and now it was streaked with blackish-red blood. Kita, wide-eyed, looked to Miaka for answers or reassurance.

She walked calmly to her daughter, took her hand, and held it to her own heart, wanting Kita to connect with the loud beating, the drum that all life marched to. And even though her own mind was filled with a frightening darkness, she smiled and told Kita not to be afraid.

Operation Crossroads
THIRTY-NINE

The morning dew had not yet evaporated from the previous night's freshly cut grass in the courtyard of the military compound. The rocket stood poised, ready for the upcoming launch. Several gulls flew over and past the radar ball that Mr. Bachman was looking at through his classroom window.

His third-period students were just finishing a test when the bell rang. As the students began to file out of class, Mr. Bachman turned and said, "I need Carrie, Billy, Roger, Gina, Adam, and Tess to stay, please." They all sat back in their chairs and waited patiently for the others to leave before Mr. Bachman spoke.

"None of you passed this exam," he said as he waved a handful of papers in the air.

"Obviously you didn't study. I'm guessing you've been preoccupied with thoughts of war and radiation, which is probably my fault, not to mention all that Billy's brother Ted has been feeding you from the mainland."

Billy spoke out of turn.

"Yeah, well, Ted won't be *feeding* us anything else for a while. He got drafted."

Several of them moaned and sunk in their chairs.

Mr. Bachman's energy shifted.

"I'm sorry, Billy. I really hate to hear that."

He slowly walked to the front of the class, then turned to face them.

"I want you all to know that I'm giving you extra credit for going on the field trip last Saturday. Maybe that'll help balance out your grades." He held up the tests once more. "I'd still like to see you retake this test, however."

Adam raised his hand, and Bachman acknowledged him.

"Mr. B, wasn't that old woman on the island the one in the photograph on your wall?"

Mr. Bachman nodded and said, "Yes. Miaka. Our division helped her family get off the island after the Bravo test. I've kept tabs on her and her family ever since. Nine years earlier, I was a crewman on the USS Sumner."

From Billy's reaction you could tell this rang a bell, "Wow, really? You were on the *Sumner?*"

Bachman nodded.

Adam jumped in.

"Is that when you injured your arm?

Mr. Bachman got up slowly. He took a moment, then went over and locked the door.

"Actually, I didn't injure my arm."

He thought for a moment.

"I'm going to share something with you guys that I haven't shared with anyone."

He motioned to his arm.

"This is the reason I'm no longer a career military man. But let's not let this leave the classroom, okay?"

All curious, the students agreed.

Mr. Bachman continued, "Well, after the Baker test, within hours we were at ground zero. It was July 25, 1946, the first ever underwater nuclear test. It was called Operation Crossroads. Twenty-three thousand tons of TNT. Within seconds after the explosion, all sea life was destroyed for miles in every direction. You know, they had no idea what radiation was capable of back then, and we didn't know anything that was going on. We went aboard one of the target ships that had been placed around ground zero just ten hours after the blast."

Mr. Bachman took his arm out of its sling and began unraveling the Ace bandage that covered it.

"I just had on a pair of shorts and tennis shoes. We all went swimming in that water. There were dead fish all around. The water from the lagoon was also pulled up into the ship's condensers, and we drank that water."

Suddenly Carrie felt this was more than she was ready for, but it was already happening. An uncomfortable silence filled the room, and each tick of the clock sounded like thunder. Bachman took a deep breath and continued.

"We washed our clothes in that water. We weren't worried about it, because they told us it was harmless and we weren't in any danger whatsoever. It wasn't until a dozen or so years later that my arm and hand began to swell."

He pulled the last of the Ace bandage off his arm, revealing a horrid sight. His grossly enlarged arm and hand looked like something out of a science fiction movie. The kids were dumbfounded. Tess covered her eyes while Gina covered her mouth. Mr. Bachman cut into the dead silence.

"There's no question in my mind that Operation Crossroads caused this. Not just to me, but to thousands of other men. A lot of them worse off than me. Many are dead, and to this day nobody really knows for sure what caused their deaths."

Students were beginning to gather in the hall outside for the next period. Mr. Bachman quickly began to rewrap his arm and hand.

"Gets you thinking, how something that happened so long ago can still have repercussions for so many today." Bachman paused for a moment, "Again, I'd appreciate it if we can keep this on the QT, okay? Just between us."

They all agreed. As Mr. Bachman opened the door he remembered something.

"Oh, and listen, one more thing. My buddy Tom is a pilot. He offered to take all of us up on Saturday in his F4U Corsair trainer. I think we could all do with blowing off some steam. Anyone interested?"

They all nodded. Mr. Bachman had already become much more than a history teacher to them. But after today, he had securely anchored a permanent position in all of their hearts.

That Saturday, they met Mr. Bachman and his buddy Tom Borchard at the airstrip. Tom was a pilot Bachman had known since his Navy days. He taxied the F4U Corsair trainer up to the group on the Kwajalein runway and got out while it warmed up. Tom had managed to have the rare two-seater trainer shipped out to him on the island, and it was his pride and joy. The plane was bright blue and looked like a big toy idling on the runway. Mr. Bachman introduced the students to Tom, then pulled out a camera and assembled them all for a picture in front of the airplane.

The first to go up was Adam, who couldn't stop laughing as Tom did a series of barrel rolls in the Corsair. Adam looked back over his shoulder and saw Kwajalein spin full circle in the background. This was way better than any roller-coaster ride, Adam thought.

Next, Roger held on tight as Tom did a series of touch-and-goes from the runway. Roger flashed the peace sign to the awaiting group as they made another pass.

It was now Carrie's turn. She tapped Tom on the shoulder and said, "I wanna go really, really fast."

Tom replied, "Sure thing. Hang on."

As Tom throttled all the way up, Carrie closed her eyes and sat back as the plane accelerated to full speed. The two fourteen-cylinder engines each drove 1,450 horsepower to each three-blade, variable-pitch propeller. They passed the airfield at a whopping 470 miles per hour, which thrilled the group.

Billy climbed in and strapped down. They were in the air all of three minutes when Billy began to turn green. Tom looked over his shoulder and did a double-take.

"Hey, don't hurl in my cockpit! I'll get ya down."

Billy weakly disembarked the Corsair, holding his stomach, while the others tried to keep from laughing.

Mr. Bachman was the last to go up. They swung in low to buzz the kids; Bachman waved from the cockpit, and all the kids waved back. Mr. Bachman yelled to Tom over the roar of the engines.

"Tom, this was great! Thanks so much for the joy rides! These kids really needed this, and I can tell they loved it!"

Tom smiled and replied, "It's been my pleasure. I'll let you buy me a beer or two at the Yuk one of these nights."

They shared a smile as Tom banked the F4U Corsair trainer against a burning sunset and returned to the base.

Kino and Kita

FORTY

The following morning on Likiep, Kino awoke to complete silence. For a brief moment it was surreal, and he felt at peace looking up at the beams of sunlight streaming in through the holes of the thatched hut. He slowly tilted his head to share the morning with Kita, but her cot was empty, and there was a good amount of blood on it. Fear fueled him as he sprang up and ran out the open door, but Kita was nowhere in sight.

"Kita! Kita!" he yelled as panic set in. He began running through the still-sleeping village, calling her name over and over again. It was much too early for anyone to have greeted the morning.

As he turned in all directions, horrible thoughts raced through his head. *Where would she go? Is she having the baby? My god, she could be dying!*

"*Kita!*" he yelled again.

Rubbing her eyes, Miaka emerged from her hut as Kino raced past her and quickly disappeared into the dense jungle, yelling Kita's name.

His bare feet were carrying him as fast as he could run across the thick jungle floor as he scanned for her in every direction. His heart was pounding.

He came upon a clearing where there were only sparse trees. In the distance he could see a figure. It was a woman sitting completely still against a tree, with her back to him. He was sure it was Kita. He prayed to God, "Oh please, let her be okay," as he ran to her.

"*Kita!*" He saw her as he came closer. She moved slowly, and he knew she was alive. He could also see a newly dug hole in the ground in front of her.

"Kita!" He said breathlessly as he reached her. She had wrapped something in her robe, and it was bundled up on her lap. Kino's heart sank.

Kita looked at him with tired eyes and slowly began to unwrap the robe. To Kino's amazement and relief, she held up and presented him with a beautiful, healthy baby girl.

He knelt down slowly, and his entire body began to shake. He touched the newborn gently and lightly kissed her on the forehead. His emotions let go. They held each other as the baby let out a faint cry. It was over; Kino had been blessed. His girls were going to be fine.

A moment later Miaka found Kita and Kino. Through his tears Kino smiled and said, "Mama, you have a healthy granddaughter!" Miaka gratefully fell to her knees and held them both for a long time. She let all of her fears escape as they were replaced with joy and relief. Minutes later, the village doctor arrived, cut the umbilical cord, and cleaned up Kita and the baby. Several other villagers showed up with a makeshift cot. Shortly thereafter, Kita and her perfect family were on their way home.

A Hard Pill to Swallow
FORTY-ONE

Ever since the joy rides that Mr. Bachman had provided for the kids, Carrie had been feeling a little bit better. There was something about being up in Tom's plane, and that total freedom and sense of wonder that she'd felt while up in the air, that had injected her with some renewed hope for the future. She was actually looking forward to hanging out with her friends again.

She stopped in the Teen Center and still walking with a slight limp, ambled past Nestor, who was standing behind the counter, looking through some paperwork. She plopped down into the first available chair.

"Hi, Nestor."

Nestor looked up.

"Hey, Carrie. How you feet feeling today? Coral not very friendly, eh?"

Carrie was checking out the cover on the latest issue of *Seventeen* magazine and mindlessly she answered, "No, it's not."

Nestor wasn't sure if he should even bring it up; he didn't want to upset her, but he thought it was the respectful thing to do. "I so sorry about Mig. He was good guy."

Carrie leafed through the magazine, not responding or even acting like she heard.

He continued, "Sometime tings make no sense." He walked over to the community bulletin board and pulled down a flyer.

"Like dis. Have you heard? Student bring over from high school dis morning." He handed it to her. She took the flyer from him and began reading it.

Attention: All history students of Kwajalein High School: Effective immediately Mr. Bachman will be replaced by Mrs. Dreyerman. She is looking forward to meeting you all on Monday.

Carrie tossed the flyer to the floor in protest.

"No! Why?"

Nestor shook his head. "Like I say, sometimes tings make no sense."

Carrie felt like she was forever taking one step forward and two steps back. It seemed to her that the losses kept building.

She wondered why he had been let go, but she was pretty sure it had something to do with Bachman taking the kids to Likiep. She felt a twinge of guilt run through her, thinking that they might have cost Bachman his job. But then her guilt quickly turned to anger. *Assholes,* she thought.

"I can't believe they would do this. He's such a great teacher. Why would they take his job away?" Carrie got up, kicked the flyer aside, and started to leave, but Nestor stopped her.

"Carrie, your Mr. Bachman be okay. I no tink for him it matter what they take away, as much as what he give to all of you."

Carrie squeezed Nestor's hand, thanked him, and turned around to leave. It was still a hard pill to swallow, but Carrie felt appreciative as she was coming to realize why Mr. Bachman had come into their lives.

White Christmas

FORTY-TWO

Carrie sat in the back row at the Richardson Theater, staring past the screen as another mindless episode of *McHale's Navy* played. Roger knew his sister was still a bit raw from all she had been going through, but he didn't know how to reach her at times like these.

Once, when she had gotten sick in middle school, she had to miss a field trip to Catalina with all her friends. She was so disappointed and sad that she moped around the house all day. When Roger got home from school, he blew off playing football and instead initiated a marathon game of Monopoly with Carrie to keep her company. They had a blast that day, and it meant a lot to Roger that she had never forgotten it.

Hugs were rare in the Conroy household, but nonetheless, that's exactly what Roger wanted to give her. But he couldn't do it here in front of all her friends, and besides, it would have been awkward no matter what. He could tell she was uninterested in the movie and thought that perhaps Scout had something else to project on that damn screen other than *McHale's Navy.*

Roger and Adam entered the projectionist booth.

"Hey dudes, what's happening?" Scout asked.

"Not much," Roger replied.

"Hey, I know you don't have squat here worth watching, but you've gotta have something besides *McHale's Navy,* man. I think we're all pretty sick of seeing anything military."

Scout got up and began flipping through the reels of film on the shelf unit behind the projector.

"Really don't have much, man. I got a Heckle and Jeckle cartoon, a science movie—*Zinc Oxide and You*—or a Christmas flick. Take your pick."

Roger and Adam looked at each other and said in unison, "The Christmas flick."

Within a few minutes, *White Christmas* began to roll. Carrie saw this and looked over at Roger, knowing that he had just been in the projectionist's booth. Roger smiled at Carrie and gave her a thumbs-up. A slight smile tugged at the corner of Carrie's mouth. It was small, but it was enough for Roger to know he had done something to take his sister away from her pain, even if it was only a temporary fix.

Concealed inside the brown paper bag finding its way down the aisle was a pint bottle of Old Crow. The bottle was passed to Tess and then to Gina, and it continued on down, being handed off to Adam and Roger, who each took a good swig. Roger got up and walked the bottle back to Carrie, who took several good pulls off of it. Nothing like some good holiday cheer with a Christmas movie, she thought, even if it was only September.

Tess whispered to Gina, "Did you hear about Bachman?"

"Yeah, that's really fucked up," Gina said.

"Hey, and can you believe it? Carrie graced us with her presence." Tess pointed out Carrie in the other row.

Gina bent forward to see.

"Yeah, I know." She looked back to Tess.

"Hey, have you heard from Donna lately?"

Tess nodded.

"Yeah, she hates living at my grandma's. Plus, that prick Ryan hasn't contacted her once. She's written him a ton of letters and he's never even written her back. Sad thing is, she still thinks he will."

Gina noticed Ryan in the theater.

"Speak of the devil, look who's here."

Ryan emerged from the back of the dark theater, nosing around. Adam, who had just gotten the bottle back from Carrie, saw Ryan and tucked it under his shirt as Ryan walked past them on his way to get some popcorn.

Carrie was engrossed in the film and didn't even notice Ryan. It was snowing in the movie scene, and Carrie was becoming mesmerized. The buzz from the alcohol, along with the musical soundtrack, had Carrie's imagination going. Instead of the actors in the movie, she imagined the children of Rongelap playing in the snow, but it was fallout snow. She closed her eyes tight, trying to make it go away.

"How ya doing?" came a whisper in the dark that startled her abruptly and brought her out of it.

She jumped and let out a slight scream that turned a few heads. Ryan was crouched down next to her. Repulsed by his presence, she immediately moved to another seat away from him without reply, and Ryan fell back into the shadows.

By the end of the movie, Carrie had polished off the last of the Old Crow and set the bottle on the floor, just as General Waverly's end scene came on in *White Christmas.*

Bing Crosby and the other enlisted soldiers were beginning to sing to the General, *Because we love him, we love him,* and thoughts of Mig flashed through Carrie's mind. She imagined the General to be Mig in the film as the song played out. Tears began streaming down her cheeks as she watched the scene that now starred Mig. Suddenly, she felt a hand on her shoulder.

"Carrie, are you okay?" Ryan inquired again.

Carrie jumped up out of her seat and lost it.

"Don't touch me! *Get the fuck away from me!*"

All heads turned, and Roger sprang to his feet. Ryan quickly stood, throwing his hands up as if to imply he hadn't touched her. Carrie turned and stormed out of the theater, letting out a loud gasp as an uncontrollable chill racked her entire body.

"Ugh!"

Carrie's friends all got up and ran after her. Outside the theater, Billy was sitting all by himself and noticed the commotion. He jumped to his feet and followed them down to the beach. They were all trying to catch up with her. As she got to the shoreline, Adam called to her.

"Carrie, stop."

Carrie turned, and with clenched fists and through gritted teeth, she unloaded.

"I just… I just… I'm sick and tired of this bullshit. Everywhere I turn, there's bullshit!"

She shook her hair, turned, and threw her hands into the air.

"This world is so fucked up. Why does it have to be *so fucked up?* I just—"

Gina interrupted her.

"Carrie, you're—"

"Don't fucking tell me what I am!" Carrie said, cutting her off.

Adam tried to put his arm around her and console her, but Carrie deflected it.

"Get the hell away from me!" she yelled, still out of breath from the run down to the beach.

No one said a thing. They couldn't. They knew it was hopeless to even try. They stood there looking at each other, not knowing what to do.

Adam remembered he had seen Billy when they came out of the Rich, but he didn't seem to be around. He looked back over his shoulder and saw Billy standing off by himself. Something wasn't right. They all turned around and shifted their focus to Billy.

Down the shore, a good twenty feet away, was Billy, holding an envelope in his hand. Adam slowly walked over and stood in front of him. Billy extended his arm and handed the envelope to Adam. Billy's eyes were beginning to pool. The others slowly came over and gathered around. When Billy spoke, they could hear the lump in his throat.

"It's from my brother Ted's Army division."

"It's still sealed," Adam said.

"Why haven't you opened it?"

"It's addressed to my parents. I shouldn't. I can't," Billy said as a tear slipped off his cheek.

"I'm too scared."

Tess raised her hands to her face and whispered to herself, "Oh, no." She moved to Billy's side and held him as Adam slowly opened the letter. The group closed in around Billy. Carrie was the last to join. They all surrounded him as Adam began to read aloud.

"Dear Mr. and Mrs. James, it is with our deepest regret—"

Billy felt his knees buckle beneath him, but his friends were there to catch him. He pulled in a long, shuddering breath as his brow furrowed.

"Fuck!" he cried as emotions took him over.

Adam fought back his emotions as he continued to read.

"...that we have to inform you that your son, Private Theodore James, has been killed in action. We are sorry to have to—"

Billy swiped the letter out from Adam's hands before he could finish it and pulled himself away from the group. He couldn't hear this. He walked off, and under his breath, he said,

"This is so fucked up. This is *so* fucked up."

They were about to go after him, but Roger physically stopped them and said,

"No, let him go. Just let 'im go."

They knew Roger was right. Their friend was hurting, and there was nothing they could do. As they slowly walked back home in the dark, Carrie caught up with them and let Tess put her arm around her. Carrie leaned her head on Tess's shoulder as they left the beach and the waves to crash alone in the dark.

~~~~~~

Later that night, Billy arrived home with the letter in hand. He waited out front for a while before he entered, knowing that the moment he walked through that door, his whole family's lives would be changed forever. He could see and hear his parents inside through the screen door, seated at the kitchen table having a cup of coffee. He was about to be the bearer of very bad news and now wished he hadn't intercepted the letter after all. He looked at the screen door again. Responsibility weighed heavy on him. *How can I go in there and destroy my whole family?*

That crushing reality made him break down. His audible sobs caught his parent's attention from inside and they came rushing out. Consoling, his Mother put her arm around him.

"Billy, what's the matter honey?"

Billy slowly looked up at them, and with a hopeless look on his face, hesitantly extended the letter.

Through his sobs he said, "I'm so sorry Mom."

Glancing down, she saw the official military envelope and the return address. She looked back at Billy's father, in shock. She handed it to him as she felt her insides curdle.

"My Teddy boy's gone, isn't he?" She said, holding Billy tightly now, with both arms.

His Dad scanned the letter quickly, and by the crushed look on his face, their worst fears were confirmed. Under the dim porch light, that night, they held each other and wept.

Billy's family group of four was now but one of three.

The Fourth Hole
FORTY-THREE

Things seemed to be going from bad to worse, and the news of Billy's brother, Ted, being killed in Vietnam was more than any of the group could grasp or contend with.

It was hard to read Billy; his emotions were a mixture of sadness, despondency, and outrage. He had become sullen and withdrawn. When he asked them all to meet him at the fourth hole, they weren't sure why and only hoped that it meant he wanted to rejoin the living and fall back into their easy existence of not so long ago.

They streamed in, one by one, on their bikes, and when they had all gathered by the Quonset hut, the only one missing was Billy. Gina looked around nervously. "Why do you think Billy asked us here?" She looked to the others for answers.

Within minutes Billy came walking up with a duffel bag slung over his shoulder. His stride was deliberate, and he looked like he had aged years in a matter of days. Adam saw his good friend and tried to make light of the situation.

"Hey, man, here. Have a beer." He pulled the tab off the top of the beer can and handed it to Billy.

"You okay?"

Billy shook his head.

"No, man, I'm not okay." He looked down, dropped his duffel bag to the ground, and shuffled his feet.

"I need to do something, for Ted. I don't want him to be just another one of those forgotten soldiers, you know, with a flag draped over his coffin, like that makes it okay. I'm sick of hearing this *for his country* bullshit. He can't be just another casualty. Man, to me there is no greater casualty than being forgotten, and Ted is not going to be forgotten. His death needs to stand for something."

The group stood around a bit sheepishly, knowing that there wasn't anything to say. Billy reached down and picked up a rock as he continued to talk.

"This fuckin' war! We shouldn't even be fighting over there. And really, it's not just going on there—it's being fought right here. Look around man, look what we did to the Marshallese people. We destroyed their home and we destroyed them. And what about all of the American soldiers, coming home from Nam by the thousands in boxes." He tossed the rock in the direction of the rocket that was sticking up prominently behind a stand of tall trees.

Billy pounded his finger on his sternum, "Unless *we* do somethin, take some kind of stand, tell 'em it's not cool, then we're as guilty as the asshole politicians who start these fuckin' wars but don't fight 'em. Don't kid yourselves, guys—this *is* what Ted was talking about. *This* is a crisis."

Billy bent down and opened the duffel bag. Inside there was a can of spray paint, some wire cutters, and a flashlight. Adam peered inside the bag.

"What's that stuff for? What are you thinking about doing?"

Billy looked back over at the rocket. Adam knew his friend, and he could tell exactly what Billy was thinking. Adam gave him a solemn nod.

"Yeah, I guess it is pretty hot in hell." Adam looked at Roger for a beat and then back at Billy again, then said without reservation, "Fuckin' a, let's do this."

Billy pulled Roger aside.

"Roger, I need you to do something. We're gonna need a diversion. This is what I want you to do..."

Carrie wasn't sure what they were up to, but it was obvious to her that it was some wild scheme that she wanted no part of.

"What are you guys doing? You're gonna get in so much trouble!"

Billy, Adam, and Roger ignored her. Billy closed the bag and the three of them walked over to their bikes.

Tess was never one to be left out, and this appeared to be right up her alley. She wanted in.

"Hey, where are you guys going?"

The boys were already riding off.

"Guys! Wait up! Come on, you two, let's go!" she barked at Gina and Carrie.

Carrie crossed her arms defiantly.

"There's no way I'm going."

Tess had been patient with Carrie for a long time now, and she was growing tired of it. She knew Carrie had been through a lot, and so she had made every attempt to walk on eggshells so as not to upset her. But now it was Billy that needed their support, and she intended to give it to him.

"Fine, Carrie, don't come. Just stay put and don't do anything."

Tess and Gina mounted their bikes and didn't look back.

Carrie felt the sting. Something about those words were frightenly familiar and they seared her like a red-hot branding iron. But common sense dominated her thought process; if her friends wanted to do something stupid, fine, she wanted no part of it. She hastily turned her back and headed for home.

Gina and Tess pedaled fast to catch up with the boys. Tess felt her adrenalin kick in, and the energy was exciting. She started singing her favorite Cream song, *bomp bomp bomp, bomp-bomp-bomp, I feel free,* and Gina joined in, off-key.

Roger peeled down Lagoon Street, heading back home, while the girls continued to follow Billy and Adam as they made their way to the Teen Center.

When they arrived and parked their bikes, Billy glanced over at the girls.

"Stay here. We'll be right back."

Billy and Adam walked into the Teen Center, with Billy in the lead. Before entering the building, he turned to Adam and instructed him, "Okay, now. As cool as Nestor is, we can't tell him what we're doing." Adam gave Billy a nod, and they proceeded through the front door.

Nestor saw the boys as they entered. He was happy to see them, especially Billy, since he hadn't seen him since he heard of Ted's death. He had wanted to reach out earlier, but he knew that at times like this, it was best to give a person his privacy, some time to grieve on his own.

Nestor approached Billy slowly and extended his arms to give him a hug.

"Billy, so sorry to hear about your brother. Glad you came in today—I want to give you someteen."

Nestor reached in his pocket, pulled out a Saint Christopher medal on a chain, and handed it to him.

"Here, I've had this my whole life. Saint Christopher protector of safe travels. Now I think he need travel with you."

Billy was moved. Taking the chain, he replied, "Whoa, you've had this your whole life? I don't know what to say."

Nestor patted him on the back.

"No say anything. Nothing you can say. Nothing any of us can say. I no know your brother, but if he anything like you, he was good guy."

Billy choked up and found it hard to speak.

"Yeah, he was. It doesn't seem real." Billy looked off into the distance for a moment. He wanted to share a piece of his brother with Nestor, who had been like a brother to him here on the island.

"You know," said Billy, "I'll never forget this one time when we were on the beach together, sitting around a campfire, roasting marshmallows. Ted was with his friends and a couple of girls, and he had to drag me along that night. I was maybe eight or nine, and Ted kept telling me, 'Billy, don't put your marshmallow so close. It will catch on fire. To toast it perfectly, you have to roll it and keep it just the right distance away.' Yeah, he had marshmallow roasting down to a science. But I didn't listen to him, and I held it too close, and it burst into flames. I swung my stick over to Ted with the flaming marshmallow and said, 'Oh, crap. Blow out my marshmallow, Ted,' but it was so hot, it slipped right off the tip of the stick and landed flat on Ted's cheek. He let out this scream and had to peel the burning white goop off his face. I felt so bad. His cheek was bright red for the rest of the night."

Nestor had to laugh at his story.

"Did he forgive you?"

Billy smirked.

"No, man, he chased me down and pounded my ass."

Adam, who was standing at Billy's side, laughed hard at this. Billy placed the Saint Christopher around his neck and looked up at Nestor.

"Thanks, Nestor. This means a lot. Hey, can I ask you a favor?"

Nestor would have done just about anything for Billy, and he told him so. He felt a deep connection and concern, and if there was anything he could do for Billy to help ease even just an ounce of his pain, he wouldn't hesitate.

Billy told Nestor how he wanted to do a little something to honor Ted, kind of like what they had done before on the runway. What they needed was for Nestor to keep Ryan occupied and out of their hair. Nestor was more than happy to help; he told Billy not to worry, he would think of something.

Billy was relieved. So far, so good. The first step in his plan had been put into action, and with Nestor's help, he felt it would all come off without a hitch.

~~~~~

After the boys left the center, Nestor sat and contemplated how he could keep Ryan busy that night. He thought of one plan after another but couldn't think of anything that wouldn't raise Ryan's suspicion. He knew Ryan liked to have his nose in everything that went on, especially if it involved someone breaking the rules. Ryan liked to be around to implement those rules—he liked having a chance to throw his weight around a bit.

It took Nestor some doing, but he finally came up with an idea and rode over to the military base to alert Ryan to a situation where his presence might be needed. When Ryan came down to the guard shack, Nestor was there, waiting.

"Officer Ryan, I was informed that someone put shark in pool at bachelor barracks. Need to get it out."

Ryan acted irritated.

"What? Again?" This had happened before, and it was quite a feat to capture the shark and take it back out to the ocean side of the island. Ryan would love to get his hands on those pranksters.

Nestor asked Ryan if he could help or get someone to assist, and Ryan assured him that he would round up a couple of MPs and that together they would take care of it. Nestor thanked Ryan, then turned and rode back to the Teen Center, wearing a smile that stretched from ear to ear.

R.I.P.
FORTY-FOUR

Carrie threw herself on her bed and covered her eyes with both hands, wanting to black out the world completely. She wished she could have a do-over, as she hated the way she had become estranged from her friends and knew full well that she was losing them. She tried to forget and carry on, but her world had changed so drastically that she didn't know how to put it back together. But God, her heart hurt, and she missed all of them.

Tess and Gina seemed to be growing closer, while Carrie was on the distant sidelines. It had hurt when Tess made that terse remark, "Don't do *anything*, Carrie." It was true. Carrie had basically given up; she didn't care, and nothing really seemed worth fighting for. Not her friendships, and at times, not even her own life.

Carrie thought of Billy, and then it hit her, hard. My God, she shivered, Billy had just lost his brother. She remembered the gut wrenching grief and helplessness that she had felt when learning her own sister was dead.

Carrie looked over at her bookcase. Her eyes settled on a photo of Sara and Roger. It was one taken on a family vacation to New York, and Sara was posing like the Statue of Liberty, standing stiff, straight faced and using her dripping vanilla ice cream cone as the torch. Her brother Roger was posed, licking the dripping ice cream running down her arm. It had always made Carrie laugh.

The photo next to it was taken one Christmas morning. Carrie and Sara sat together, cross-legged on the floor, in front of the lit up tree. They were wearing their new matching pajamas and drinking hot chocolate out of Rudolph the Red-Nosed Reindeer mugs, the kind where Rudolph's red shiny nose actually blinked off and on. Their radiant little faces had put the Christmas tree lights to shame.

Carrie sat up on the edge of her bed. She caught her reflection in the dresser mirror across the room. Instantly she was tossed back in time, to that horrible night when she sat, just like this, on the edge of her parent's bed, waiting for Sara to return, but never did. The same feeling swept through her body, that same tightness that had gripped her before, rendering her useless and too scared to move.

No! She heard in her own head. *Get up!*

The same old questions racked her mind. What if she didn't just sit there that night, what if she'd gone out to see what was going on? She didn't want to think about it, but what if? Sara might very well still be alive.

Ever since Sara was murdered, Carrie had lost her way. Her once confident self had been left feeling shaky and insecure. Like a runaway train, she felt out of control, and had no idea where she was headed. It was as if she were lying on the railroad tracks, just waiting to be run over. As she started to toss out blame and find someone she could point a finger at, it instantly became clear to her, that *she* had been the one holding herself captive. It was *she* that had tied *herself* to those tracks and all she needed to do was to get up and get out of her way. With that realization, a lightness and energy infused her.

Carrie sprang from the bed and stood straight up. Her body told her to move; her head asked her, to where? She looked out the window, back at her bed, and over to the desk chair, where the peace sign T-shirt that she had silk-screened in Bachman's class was draped across the back. Her eyes locked in on the shirt and the peace sign. Then it hit her, and without a doubt, she now knew what she had to do.

Carrie quickly slipped on her sandals, and tore through her closet, looking for her old canvas shoulder bag. She rummaged through her desk drawer, searching for a black Magic Marker. Grabbing her T-shirt off the chair, she spread it as evenly and as flatly as she could across the bed and began to write across the front of it. When she finished, she held it up, admired her handiwork, smiled, and let out a big "Yesss!"

She shook the shirt for a minute to dry the ink, and then pulled it on over her head. She tossed the marker in her bag, ran out to her waiting bike, and took off at full speed.

Billy, Adam, and Roger had arrived at the military base, and they paced outside the ominous chain-link fence that surrounded it. There was a moment when they all seemed to wonder if they should just head back to the fourth hole and down a few cold ones. But then Billy opened up his duffel bag, removed the spray paint can and a flashlight, and stuffed them in his pockets. He retrieved the wire cutters from the bag and prepared to cut the chain-link fence. Looking at Adam, he whispered, "Anyone coming that direction?"

Adam turned his head to check.

"Looks clear here," he whispered back.

Billy looked over at Roger.

"What about your way? How's it look?"

Roger looked around.

"The coast is clear."

Billy turned back to the fence and under his breath he muttered, "Here goes nothin'."

Just as he touched the wire cutters to the fence, a loud siren began to wail. Freaked, Billy dropped the wire cutters. Adam and Roger grabbed Billy and forcefully tackled him to the ground. Quickly scrambling to their feet, they started to run, but Billy stopped.

"Wait," he said in a hushed voice, "that's the evening siren, you morons."

Adam and Roger looked at each other and busted up laughing. Billy shot them a serious look and they tried hard to regain their composure.

Billy picked up the cutters again and slowly approached the fence. He crouched down and began carefully cutting through the galvanized aluminum. After each snip with the cutters, he curled back the razor sharp ends. Once creating a trash can size hole, he removed the chain link center and tossed it over into the bushes. He looked up at Adam with a wry smile and gave him a firm thumbs up.

Just then Tess and Gina arrived and joined up with Adam and Roger. Billy was glad they had come. There was comfort in numbers.

He looked hard at all his friends. He was ready. "Okay, Roger, let's double-check our time," Billy said. They synced their watches. Billy patted Roger on the back.

"Hey, Roger, thanks. And when you get done, get the hell out of there, and we'll catch up with you later."

Roger gave a little laugh.

"No way, man, I'll be back here before you know it. You think I'd miss this action?"

Billy looked at the others and said, "Okay, let's go."

Just then a bike could be heard coming up the crunchy gravel road. Everyone stopped. Tess was the first to see her. "Carrie!" she cried out, much louder than Billy would have liked.

Carrie jumped off her bike and let the weight of her bag slip off her shoulder. She walked up to the group, wearing the peace sign T-shirt with her newly added lettering. Without saying a word, she reached in the bag and handed them each their own, with the very same alterations.

Above the peace sign Carrie had written in black marker, "REST IN," and below the peace sign she had written, "TED." (*Rest in Peace Ted*)

Gina looked at her shirt.

"Wow, Carrie, this is so cool."

Adam tore off the shirt he was wearing and pulled his new T-shirt over his head, shaking his hair as he smoothed the shirt across his chest.

"How'd you pull this off?"

Carrie just smirked and replied, "Easy. No one locks their doors on Kwaj."

Billy took the shirt and proudly held it up for everyone to see. He felt a wave of love go through him for Carrie and for all of his friends. He pulled off his old white tee and put on his new RIP Ted shirt. Patting his chest, he said, "Thanks, Carrie. Welcome back." The midnight raiders now had their own uniforms.

Tess was proud of Carrie and thrilled to have her back. She gave Carrie a big hug and whispered in her ear, "You did good."

Roger gave a salute to Billy as he sped off to his post, while the remaining four carefully followed Billy through the jagged hole into the base compound.

Shark Attack
FORTY-FIVE

Ryan was pissed off that he had to spend the evening running over to the bachelor pool, and at the same time he was excited that he had the opportunity to exercise his minimal authority.

The last time this happened, they never did catch the perpetrators, and this maddened Ryan to no end. Not only did it make him look bad, but also he had really wanted to put those teenagers (he assumed) in their place.

The last time it had been quite a fiasco, taking what seemed like hours trying to catch the shark while entertaining the growing number of jeering spectators. Once they had the shark contained, they had placed it in the back of a pickup truck and continually dumped buckets full of water on him until they could safely release it out near the shark pit. Not this time, Ryan thought. He intended to make quick work of this.

Ryan and the MPs arrived at the barracks with guns drawn. Several residents had already gathered around, as if at a circus. Ryan had made the decision on the ride over that he wasn't going to waste time trying to capture the damn creature; he was just going to take it out. It wasn't often that Ryan or any MP, for that matter, actually got to pull the trigger of a gun, except at target practice, and this would be one of those very rare occasions where he could do it. He savored the moment, feeling the power of the cold steel in his hand, an extension of himself, making him feel like the hero he never was.

Ryan held the spectators at bay and charged up to the pool area, where he could see the gray and white shark surfacing from a distance. Rashly he took aim and fired, and immediately upon impact there was a loud, startling pop, followed by a hiss, causing the crowd to roar in knee-slapping laughter.

Ryan's concentration was blown, and he wasn't sure what had just happened. Looking from the crowd back to the pool, he could see a deflated, shriveling plastic shark floating on top of the clear blue pool water.

Enraged, Ryan turned angrily back to the MPs, who stood behind him, trying to maintain their composure. His face flushed red as he commanded, "Come with me. Heads are going to fuckin' roll!"

~~~~~~

Nestor found himself worried about Billy and the rest of the gang. He hadn't even thought to ask Billy what exactly he had planned; he had been so focused on providing him a bit of help, a little relief. He hoped that he hadn't agreed to help him with anything bigger, like the places his imagination was now taking him.

Billy had said something about sending a message, like the one he had done before. Even though Billy had never admitted to painting the peace sign on the runway, everyone pretty much assumed it was him… with, of course, a little help from his friends.

Nestor closed up the Teen Center and decided to ride over and make sure they were okay and that they weren't getting into anything that they might later regret.

He rode at a fast clip, with the warm evening wind blowing against his face. As Nestor coasted past the runway, there was no sign of any of the kids or their bikes. Everything looked in order. He stopped for a moment, and his mind jumped here and there. He thought long and hard about what those kids might be up to and where they might be. He had a hunch, an uneasy feeling, and he raced over to the base.

When he got there, he got off his bike and started walking the perimeter. The floodlights were glaring, but it seemed quiet. His eyes caught the reflection of some jagged wire, and upon closer inspection he could see that an actual hole had been cut in the fence, a hole large enough for a person to slip through.

"Oh, no mon, this can't be good," Nestor mumbled to himself. He squinted his eyes and tried to peer through, but the glare of the floodlights against the shiny silver rocket made it hard to see.

But Nestor didn't need to see, for his intuitive vision was much clearer, and he knew that he had found them.

The Ascent

FORTY-SIX

Getting caught inside a military perimeter was risky business, especially for a bunch of teenagers with a spray paint can who intended to scale a nuclear rocket. If a little paint on the runway caused such a stink, how would the Commanding General react to this act of trespassing and vandalism? But such thoughts were not at the forefront of Billy's mind. His only thoughts were of Ted and what he stood for, and carrying out his brother's pledge for peace.

Covertly they inched their way deeper and deeper into the base compound. Carrie couldn't help but think, *This is so crazy. There's helping a friend, and then there's doing something really stupid.* She knew that being there and supporting her friends was of paramount importance, but also wondered if she was the only one who was sane. But there was no going back, and now Carrie could feel her heart beginning to pound deep inside of her chest. The saving grace, she thought, was that if they got caught, they would all go down together.

Darting in and out of the shadows as MPs moved by on patrol, the group made their way along. It crossed Carrie's mind that if some trigger-happy MP detected them moving through the shadows, he could justifiably shoot now and ask questions later. She shook off the thought and continued on.

Sliding in behind a fichus hedge next to an outbuilding, they finally managed to get close to the rocket. Glancing at his watch, Billy smiled; it was almost time for the diversion. A few moments passed. Nothing. Adam grabbed Billy by the arm and shook his head, indicating that he shouldn't chance it. Billy pulled loose from his grasp and gave Adam a stern look. It was clear to all of them that Billy was doing this no matter what, and nobody was going to stop him.

At that moment several huge booms shattered the night's silence, followed by an explosive burst of fireworks over the far north side of the compound.

Hiding in a construction site roughly fifty yards outside the perimeter of the missile base, Roger had begun orchestrating a brilliant fireworks diversion for Billy's mission. Roger's arsenal of fireworks included Roman candles, multi-shot cakes, air mortars, and an assortment of jumbo bottle rockets. Keeping a keen eye out for when it was time to hightail it out of there, he gave each a cursory reading of the instructions before he lit them off.

"Let's see, *Use care when lighting.* Oh, I plan to. *Always follow the law.* Well, it's a bit too late for that," he said as he aimed an air mortar over the compound and lit it off.

The blast sent Roger windmilling backward. It soared a good hundred and fifty feet into the air over the compound and exploded with a thunderous boom, surrounded by crackling purple sparkles that quickly dissipated in the night sky. He propped himself up on his elbows, and with smoldering eyebrows, he smiled and said, "Coooool!"

Mayhem broke out throughout the military base as personnel streamed outside, expecting to see the Russians invading Kwajalein. The air-raid siren began to wail, initiating a general alert for all military personnel.

Suddenly, Carrie and her friends found themselves laughing hysterically. Holding their hands over their mouths, they tried not to give up their secret position. The courtyard quickly became deserted, and Billy carefully emerged with his spray-paint can in hand and looked up at the poised rocket with a sense of awe.

Scaffolding and round girders adjoined the rocket, which was positioned for launch at a sixty-degree angle over the ocean. At the top of the scaffolding there was a small platform by the nose cone's tip. Billy sized up the task ahead of him, took a deep breath, stuffed the spray can in his front pocket, and stealthily moved to the scaffolding to begin his ascent.

Carrie and the group watched nervously as Billy's mission for his fallen brother commenced. Rapidly he began his climb with monkeylike precision, carefully planning each and every foot and hand placement on the scaffolding. At one point, about forty feet up, he slipped and dangled. Carrie held her breath. Billy, like in gym class, "kiped" himself back up onto the scaffolding, which caused the spray can to pop out of his front pocket. He instinctively tried to catch it, but gravity won. The can fell, hitting a cross brace on its way down, sounding a loud ping across the courtyard, and landed on the grass below. Leaping out from behind the fichus hedge, Carrie sprang into action. She bolted over to the spray-paint can, picked it up, and began climbing up to meet Billy.

Nestor was just walking up and saw Carrie. He found the rest of the kids hiding behind the hedge and joined them.

"What you tink you doing? You want to get yourselves killed?" he whispered sternly.

Adam held a finger to his lips, indicating for him to be quiet, as they all intently watched as Carrie made the climb, holding the spray-paint can in one hand, as Roger's fireworks display continued.

Ryan's car was nearing the base now, and he could see the fireworks.

"What the fuck?" he muttered under his breath.

Climbing within ten feet of Billy, Carrie decided to lob the can to him instead of going any farther. She leaned out to get a clear shot and carefully tossed it up to him. Billy caught it, but the bottoms of Carrie's sandals were moist from the wet grass below, and the movement caused her feet to slip from her perch on the scaffold. She scrambled to find something to hold onto, but there was only the round steel girder. She caught it and was left hanging, holding on with a strength she didn't know she possessed.

Adam ran out from the cover and jumped up on the round girder, which was roughly the circumference of a coconut tree. He began to hop up it using the technique Nestor had taught them. Nestor drew a trembling hand to his mouth as he watched from the shadows.

Carrie was losing her grip. She grimaced, looking down at Adam, straining to hold on.

"Hurry, Adam. I can't hold on much longer," she said in a panic.

Adam kept his eye fixed on Carrie, although in the back of his mind, he knew he was getting higher off the ground, which began interfering with his concentration. He looked down for a second, and fear had him. Nestor bit his lip. Adam tried to regain his momentum. He made another hop but lost his grip and fell down to the grass below.

Nestor bolted out of hiding, leaped onto the girder, and rapidly hopped up to rescue Carrie. Wrapping an arm around her waist, he pulled her back safely onto the scaffolding, where they caught their breath and exchanged grateful smiles. Billy saw she was safe and continued his ascent to the gantry.

Ryan drove his car into the base and parked. Tess and Gina saw this and tried to call to the others, but to no avail. Carrie, Nestor, and Billy were too high, and yelling to them would surely give them away.

Billy was now by the nose of the rocket, which protruded over the shark pit. He climbed out onto the gantry. Nestor indicated that he was going up to Billy and urged Carrie to go back down.

Streaming toward Roger was a wall of MPs with flashlights. Roger had just finished fashioning a long fuse that attached the remaining bundle of fireworks together. He aimed them directly at the oncoming MPs, snapped open his lighter, and lit the fuse.

"It says *Light fuse and get away*. I'd better follow the instructions," he said, chuckling to himself, and dashed off into the darkness. The fireworks exploded, sending bottle rockets, Roman candles, and a jumbo pack of pyrotechnic mortars hurling directly at the oncoming MPs. Fireworks sped past them in all directions.

The Commanding General had just picked up his assault rifle and was walking out of his office when he saw a Roman candle headed directly for him. He dove into the back of a jeep, narrowly missing being hit. The Roman candle traveled past him and through the open window of an MP latrine, exploding inside and sending personnel scattering in every direction.

Billy had begun the final step of the operation: spray-painting a message on the rocket. A spotlight somewhere in the compound snapped on, illuminated the rocket, and zeroed in on Billy. Ryan was just getting out of his car with the two MPs when this caught his attention.

"Is that one of those fucking high school idiots? Give me your weapon, soldier," he ordered. He loaded a bullet in the chamber of the Browning high-power Army service pistol and headed for the lift elevator. Ryan could now see that it was Billy on the rocket.

"Get off that rocket, Billy!" Ryan shouted. He boarded the elevator and hit the lift button. Nestor could clearly see Ryan with the gun moving up in the elevator, so he climbed up onto the gantry next to Billy, who was trying to ignore everything and focus on finishing his task.

The Sacrifice
FORTY-SEVEN

Roger's fireworks had ended and MPs began to filter back into the courtyard and gather down below with guns drawn, followed by Ryan's father, the Commanding General, who was holding his assault rifle. Several more spotlights were turned on and directed to the nose of the rocket. Roger arrived, snuck up, and found a safe hiding place. He saw his sister Carrie, who had continued to follow Nestor and was now on the scaffolding just ten feet below the gantry platform.

Ryan left the elevator, stepped out onto the gantry, and leveled the Browning on Billy and Nestor. Ryan glanced down at the MPs with their guns drawn below. "Hold your fire! I've got a clean angle on him here!"

Nestor blocked Billy, protecting him.

"That gun is no necessary, mon!" Nestor yelled.

"Stand aside, darky. This doesn't concern you," Ryan replied with a snarl on his lip.

Nestor leaned in and said, "I know your kind, Ryan, I saw you in Carrie's hospital room. You a sick mudderfucker."

Carrie heard this and searched her memory, then slowly looked up and locked eyes with Ryan. A sick smile transformed Ryan's face, and Carrie felt her insides turn and her blood begin to boil.

Ryan glanced over and could see the shark pit below. He checked the Browning for a round in the chamber and pointed the gun at Nestor, who didn't budge an inch. Carrie began to climb up the rest of the way.

Ryan took several more steps toward Nestor and said, "You can't protect these kids. You're just going to get yourself killed, you fuckin' mook."

Lurching up onto the gantry, Carrie grabbed Ryan's leg, pulling it out from under him. Ryan landed hard, causing the service pistol to slide several feet away from his grasp. He reached out for it, but Carrie was still holding onto his ankle. Ryan kicked at Carrie, sending her slipping backward off the gantry. Carrie managed to grab onto the center scaffolding support but was left dangling over the shark pit.

Nestor lunged toward Carrie, but Ryan clotheslined him with an extended arm to the throat, knocking him backward; Nestor gagged as he struggled to regain his breath. Nestor's adrenalin surged, and he grabbed Ryan in a headlock. Ryan broke free and managed to get in several haymaker-style blows. Nestor blocked the last of the incoming blows and countered with a slam to Ryan's gut, doubling him over and sending searing pain through his solar plexus.

Billy couldn't get past them, and he watched helplessly as Carrie hung precariously over the shark pit. Ryan threw a combination of punches that sent Nestor spinning backward and falling on his stomach next to the Browning. Nestor grabbed the gun and spun around, but Ryan caught his wrist, and they struggled to their feet on the gantry, vying for the Browning.

A shot rang out from below, and a hollow-point shell ripped through Ryan's side, disrupting his equilibrium. For a split second Nestor didn't know what had happened. Ryan grabbed his bleeding side, wobbled, took a step back, and slipped off.

Slamming into the scaffolding below, he managed to latch on with one hand; he now swung over the shark pit, next to Carrie. Below, slowly lowering the smoking barrel of his assault rifle, was the Commanding General.

Nestor grabbed Carrie and helped her back up onto the gantry.

"Are you okay, Carrie?" he asked, out of breath. She nodded and got to her feet.

Billy reached up and called out, "Nestor! Help me." Nestor turned and went to help Billy back onto the gantry. Carrie looked over the edge of the platform and saw Ryan hanging there, helpless.

"Carrie, please help me up. I've been shot. I can't hold on. *Please!*"

The movement of Carrie's head was almost indiscernible. Her lower eyelids raised and her look of disgust was slowly replaced by her version of Ryan's sick smile. She folded her arms, cocked her head, and said, "I don't want to leave you hanging, Ryan."

Ryan's grip slowly slipped off the scaffolding as he screamed, "Noooooooooooo!"

Carrie kept her eyes locked on his as he fell seventy-five feet into the shark pit below, creating a huge splash.

Several MPs came rushing to Ryan's aid, but with his side bleeding and his thrashing in the water, the sharks were on him in no time, human chum, dragging him down screaming into the red, swirling void.

Carrie spun around and buried her face in Nestor's chest.

An MP below spoke into a loudspeaker.

"Put your hands up over your head, or we'll fire."

Nestor took the gun, set it down on the gantry, and put his hands over his head; Carrie and Billy followed suit. The Commanding General turned to the MP next to him and ordered quietly, "Fire at will, soldier."

Nestor, Carrie, and Billy all stood frozen. A shot was fired from below, striking Nestor in the shoulder.

Carrie screamed, *"No!"*

Nestor stumbled backwards, lost his footing, and fell from the gantry. The scaffolding broke his fall and catapulted him away from the shark pit and onto the grass below. Carrie and Billy scrambled down the scaffolding to reach Nestor, who was badly broken up and bleeding. Roger, Adam, Tess, and Gina came running out. MPs surrounded the whole group as they could hear an ambulance in the distance approaching.

Carrie pressed her hand against Nestor's bleeding shoulder and said softly, "I'm so sorry. Hang in there, Nestor. An ambulance is coming." She looked down and saw his legs were badly broken.

Nestor tried to speak but could hardly get the words out. He looked at the faces of the kids he loved so much. He smiled at Adam and said weakly, "You never could climb a coconut tree, mon."

Carrie and the group stood by as the ambulance pulled up. Quickly, the paramedics lifted him onto a stretcher and loaded him into the ambulance. The paramedic hopped in the back and before he closed the door, he stopped, seeing the kid's anguished faces. "Don't worry guys," he said, "it looks like he'll pull through."

Uncharacteristically, Roger gave Carrie a long hug, he was glad his sister was safe. Just then the MPs began handcuffing the kids to lead them off.

The Commanding General and an MP stood by the shark pit, staring into the red-stained water, looking numb. There wasn't any sign of Ryan.

The MP looked at the General and said, "Sir, I'm sorry. We couldn't get to him in time."

The Commanding General slowly shook his head and said, "Neither could I, soldier. Neither could I."

Another MP walked up and said to the General, "We have a detail ready to clean off the graffiti before liftoff tomorrow, sir."

The General asked what it said, and the MP whispered something into his ear. General Mitchell looked at the MP blankly, then back at the shark pit. "Instruct the detail to stand down on the cleanup, soldier. Let it fly as is."

The Box

FORTY-EIGHT

Several days had passed and security had finished cleaning out the contents of Lieutenant Mitchell's quarters. The Commanding General was contacted to inspect his son's personal effects. When the General arrived at the bachelor's barracks he thought it was strange to see a rather large presence of military police. A bit puzzled, he saluted each officer as he approached the barracks. The General's second in command, Colonel Beckwith, met the General and expressed his condolences.

"Sir, I'm so sorry for your loss," he said as he led the General to Lieutenant Mitchell's room.

The General asked, "Colonel, what's all the police presence about?"

Colonel Beckwith paused for a moment, realizing the General had not yet been informed.

"Sir, an investigation has been opened."

The General cocked his head quizzically and said, "Colonel, my son is dead. What in the hell is there to investigate, or is this some kind of a sick joke?"

As they arrived at the door to Ryan's room it was covered with an "X" of crime scene tape that read, *Crime Scene – Do Not Cross*. The General ripped the tape down.

"What the hell is this, Colonel?" the General snapped.

The Colonel hung his head, "I'm very sorry, sir. The contents of Lieutenant Mitchell's possessions are in a box on his bed for your perusal. Take as much time as you need."

The General opened the door and entered the room. The Colonel added, "You won't be able to take it. States evidence."

At this, the General leaned in nose to nose to Colonel Beckwith and said, "There had better be a good God-damn explanation for this, Colonel."

He turned his back and entered the room. Another MP stood at attention inside the room on guard. The General walked into the bathroom and looked at himself in the shattered medicine chest mirror. He turned on his heels looking back into the room and saw a box on the bed. The bed had been stripped and the blankets and linens were folded into a neat square on the bed next to the box. The closet door was open, and Ryan's clothes were all hanging, pressed and neatly organized, with several pairs of shiny patent leather shoes on the floor.

The General sat on the bed and opened the box. He removed Ryan's service manual and a small folded wad of cash in a rubber band. Next came the men's magazine Ryan had hidden under his mattress. The General cringed and quickly put it away. A half dozen or so letters slipped out from inside the magazine. They were all addressed to Ryan from Donna. The General unfolded one and began to read it.

"Our baby is healthy and missing his father. When will you be coming home? I can't wait to see you..." The General shut his eyes tight and shook his head at the realization. He replaced it back in the envelope and put the letters aside.

The General pulled from the box a framed picture of Carrie and her family. At the bottom of the box were several newspaper clippings. The headline on the first one read:

Military   Family's   Daughter   Murdered— Investigation Surrounding Home Invasion Ongoing. Another clipping read, *Sara Conroy Murder Case, Key Eyewitness Commits Suicide—Killer At Large.*

But the most disturbing discovery came next: A hand-written letter on a folded up piece of notebook paper.

Ryan, I haven't stopped thinking about you since we last met. Since all of our parents are going to be gone on Saturday night to the base party at Camp Pendleton, I was hoping to see you again. I'll be at Sara Conroy's house all night. Let's finish what we started...

~ *Trisha Bradford*

The General rubbed his hands on his thighs and remembered back to the night after the Camp Pendleton ball in Oceanside and hearing about the Sara Conroy murder. He recollected the concern he and his wife experienced from Ryan not returning home that night and their interrogation of him that followed the next day. He knew from the bruises on Ryan's hand and the scratches on his temple and neck that the circumstances pointed to nefarious activities. The General felt overwhelmed with shame. It was now very clear that his son, Ryan, was responsible for the killing of Sara Conroy.

The General slowly got up, took a deep breath, walked back into the bathroom and quietly shut the door behind him. The MP in the room didn't think much of this until a shot rang out and the sound of a body hit the floor. The MP bolted towards the door, drawing his gun, but the General's lifeless body blocked his entrance.

The Message

FORTY-NINE

Billy sat handcuffed, sandwiched between two air marshals on the military transport. He looked out the small, scratchy, discolored window and could see his friends standing near the spectator wall, trying to catch a final glimpse of him, or at least a final glimpse of him on Kwajalein.

The Saint Christopher medal that Nestor had given him, hung around his neck. Many on the island had asked him if he regretted what he had done, and he had told them that no, he had no regrets. But that wasn't the entire truth; he did regret that he had involved Nestor and the others. He'd never intended any harm to come to any of them.

The final act had been rather half-baked, something that was fueled by raw passion, and not a lot of thought had gone into the actual consequences he and the others might face for their actions. But for Billy, the most important thing was that he had done something in the name of his brother, and in his heart he knew that he had made Ted proud.

Behind the spectator wall, Carrie raised her arm to shield the glare of the sun from her eyes, straining to catch sight of Billy through the plane's small, round window. Adam squinted hard as a flock of seagulls got spooked off the runway and flew off overhead. He turned to see them go by, but what he saw when he turned around took him by surprise. A mass of bicycles was approaching, so many that they resembled a rapidly rising tide. What looked like hundreds of kids, if not the entire student body of Kwajalein High, had assembled and come riding up to join the others at the observation area.

They all filtered in behind Adam and the others. Some of them were carrying anti-war protest signs in Billy's honor. Seeing them, Carrie felt like she was going to burst with pride. She turned back to Billy and raised her hand high above her head, giving the peace sign. Adam, Roger, Gina, and Tess did the same. In solidarity, the mass of kids raised peace signs to the sky as well.

An airman came out of the cockpit and walked up to Billy, whose head was down. He pointed out the window.

"Um, I think you might want to take a look out there."

Billy lifted his head and looked outside. He couldn't believe what he saw. There was his small group of friends, and behind them, a massive group of cheering kids that made him feel like a rock star. Billy smiled.

Not only had his message been sent, but more importantly, it had been heard. He yanked his handcuffed hand up high, pulling the annoyed air marshal's hand right up along with his, and waved vigorously to the crowd that had come to support him.

He felt a deep sense of satisfaction, now convinced that all they had gone through was not in vain. As the plane taxied down the runway and lifted off, Billy kept his friends in sight until they became like an unrecognizable abstract painting below. The plane lifted off, and Billy's stomach did a quick succession of flip-flops. He closed his eyes and then laid his head back on the seat and tried hard not to think about what kind of future awaited him as he headed back to face the consequences of his actions.

At about the same time Billy's flight reached cruising altitude, the missile had been launched from Kwajalein, and it was rapidly entering the upper atmosphere. With the General's permission, the missile still bore Billy's artful tribute to Ted.

In large block letters, there flew the message,

"WAR IS NOT HEALTHY FOR CHILDREN AND OTHER LIVING THINGS" for all, including the heavens, to see.

Going Home
FIFTY

C arrie shoved the small bag under the seat in front of her and buckled the seat belt. On this flight she had claimed the window seat. Soaring above the clouds and watching the world fall away was her favorite part of flying.

Roger was sitting across the aisle, already engrossed in a Continental Airlines magazine. Carrie felt bittersweet about leaving her incredible friends, but there was a bright note; she was finally going to see her Moe again.

She was deep in thought as she stared out the window, reliving the past three years that she had spent on the island. It was amazing to her; she felt she had gone through more in that short period than some people go through in a lifetime.

Yes, Carrie thought, life was full of surprises, some good and some bad. It had been a whirlwind. She thought about Mig and the time she'd snuck into the barracks to see him, the party at her house, Maru's red dress and that bright red lipstick, so many days and nights laughing and drinking at the fourth hole, and all the fun times they had spent with Nestor at the Teen Center.

She had to laugh, thinking about outrunning Curtis and the night he got his truck stuck between the two coconut trees. She almost felt a little sorry for him now. The waterskiing adventure when her parents were in Hawaii, and how thankful they all were that she hadn't ended up shark-bait. Of course, it was funny now, but it was terrifying at the time.

Thinking about Mr. Bachman; he was a true hero. Although he ended up losing his job after taking them to meet Miaka, he wound up doing something he was truly passionate about.

They heard from him a few months later. Back on the mainland, he had started a foundation to help the Marshallese people. It was an educational and advocacy organization where they were exposing the consequences of using nuclear weapons. And, if she and her friends happened to play any small part in helping Mr. Bachman realize his true passion, she felt pretty damn good about that—there might even be a place for a young, ambitious intern with Mr. B's organization sometime in the future.

And then, at the other end of the spectrum, there was the unbelievable investigation surrounding Mig's death where it was revealed that he had died from carbon monoxide poisoning. But how it happened, had remained an unsolved mystery until testimony from Rudy, Mig's diving partner, came forward. Rudy had stated that they had only been down for a few minutes before he brought Mig back to the surface, therefore his air tank would have been relatively full. When Ryan offered to retrieve Mig's aqualung from the cabin of Mig's boat, Rudy thought it was odd that Ryan didn't come immediately back out with the aqualung. And then, when he finally did, he remembered thinking that the tank now seemed lighter and noticed by the gauge, it was empty. This could only mean one thing; while Ryan was alone in the cabin, he released the remainder of the tainted air in the tank and therefore incriminated himself.

How was it possible that one man could take away her sister and the first man she ever loved? It seemed so unfathomable. How ironic it was, moving away only to find that Sara's killer had moved right along with them. Knowing he had been on the island, living among them the entire time, still sent chills down her spine. Carrie was glad he was dead. It had been a nightmare. Finding out that Ryan was responsible for Sara's death had at least helped her and her family breathe a little easier, and to get a little closure, even though Carrie knew you could never really close the door on the loss of a loved one.

And in the same way that she would never get over losing Sara and Mig, she knew Billy would never get over losing Ted. She was just happy that in her small way she had been there for him when he needed her most. They all had. And they had all been there for her, too. She couldn't have asked for more loyal friends.

Just then the stewardess leaned in and asked, "Can I get you something to drink, sweetie?" Carrie nodded and asked for a Fresca. The stewardess filled the little plastic cup with ice, poured the soft drink to the brim, and handed it back to her with a napkin and a bag of macadamia nuts.

"Bet you're happy to be moving back to the States," said the stewardess.

"I can't imagine there's much happening on a small island like Kwaj."

Carrie stared at the woman blankly, turned to look out the window, and smiled to herself.

Carrie sat there thinking, since her arrival on the island in 1969, it seemed like the whole country had grown up so fast—right before her very eyes, and she and her friends had all grown up right along with it.

All that they had been through, all the lessons that they really didn't want to learn, had brought them to where they were today. She was filled with an awareness of the rights and wrongs of the world, but also the satisfaction that, in the end, they hadn't remained neutral, they took a stand and tried to make a difference. And in doing so, they had avoided the hottest places in hell.

Carrie giggled and thought to herself, it sounds so crazy, but who knows, you wake up one morning feeling passionate about some injustice or something that isn't right, and the next thing you know, you find yourself holding a can of spray paint and scaling a rocket.

About The Authors

When Michael Bayouth, of Woodland Hills, California, found out that his writing partner, Kim Klein, of Santa Barbara, California, had lived on a tiny island, ½ mile wide by 3 miles long in the middle of the Pacific, on a missile base called *Kwajalein*, he told her he had never even heard of the place. Michael and Kim quickly realized that this was not only a great coming of age story but it became much more significant due to the setting, the ongoing Vietnam War, and the tumultuous atomic era.

So they started their endeavor and simultaneously started a Facebook page to draw in some of the stories for inspiration from several of Kim's Kwajalein classmates. A mere week and a half later, after roughing out the outline, they had over 400 members on the Facebook page, which continues to grow to this day. This obviously filled their sails and *Nine Degrees North* exploded onto the page.

Award-winning author Kim Klein has written for several newspapers and has authored a variety of very popular blogs. She does freelance editorial consulting, specializing in writing and research. Her passion for writing is complemented by her experience in a variety of fields, such as Feng Shui, Chinese medicine, multi-media art and design. She is currently working on a novel, *Letters from York*.

Born into Hollywood, Michael Bayouth is a guy who early on developed a passion for storytelling, design and expression. He sees the world in a unique and visual way – something that his work expresses in a range of settings – from writing and directing to storyboarding and graphic design to production design, animation, and more. His passion is to create stories to move people emotionally, and he brings energy and life to everything he produces.

Michael Bayouth's flare for writing, directing and producing can be seen in the mockumentary *Take 22*, his debut comedy feature film for exhibition, which won BEST PICTURE and BEST ACTOR awards at the Raleigh Motion Picture Studios in Hollywood California during Mock Fest. The feature film was nominated for FIVE awards.

His Graphic Arts Design can be seen on the seventh season of NBC's hit series *The Office* while his *Johnny Bananas* characters were showcased throughout many episodes of HBO's hit series *Entourage*.

Bayouth has 40 years experience in various creative areas of the entertainment industry. For the past 20 years, Michael Bayouth has run his own Entertainment Agency, Bayouth Productions, Inc., (www.bayouth.com) which specializes in entertainment art, advertising and servicing clients, among them Disney and Universal. Through Son of Jason Productions, Michael Bayouth's film production company, he's produced and directed 4 feature films to date, as well as many live-action shorts. (www.sonofjason.com) Michael is a member of The Writer's Guild of America, The Art Director's Guild and a lifetime member at The Magic Castle in Hollywood California.

The authors chose to create and write *Nine Degrees North* in the serene beach community of Carpinteria, California. Look for this project on Facebook at, *Facebook.com/NineDegreesNorth*

Kim Klein A place for friends of Kwajalein to contribute their stories, memories and anecdotes for the "900 Miles North" movie project.

Mark Tietz u 2 are awesome and funny! u have me hook, line and sinker! kwaj was my childhood! k –12grade, minus 5th and 6th grade. i was a grad from the class of 75! the bond kwaj kids have is something special and hard 2 explain. but every kwaj kid understands it!! thanks 4 your projects!

Catherine Crash Castelli Persello We are a lucky select group. keep the happy memories close to your hearts. It's where the REAL Kwaj lives on. In our hearts, and then shared with each other. We are a special "soul group" together. I visit Kwaj quite often. I dream of Kwaj a couple of times a month. My last dream, 3 nights ago, I walked from ocean side down to my house (416–B) and around the neighborhood a little. At the far end of my street was George Seitz Elementary. But that tunnel hallway was gone. I mostly dream of moving there and working as a nurse in the hospital. But then I remember that I have a family.....

Vicki Vann Pack Whatever it is Kim we still lived there loved it and know it was really close to the equator!!!! I know that piece you wrote touched each and everyone one of us as I know that's exactly how I felt!! I went to Kwaj in June of 69 and we were on a prop plane....took us 10 hours with a refueling stop on Johnston Island. That's when I really wondered just where in the world was I going !!!

Tom Zebal Altair supposedly could tell the RPM of all the 4 engines (prop plane) on the incoming flights from HONO – and – via computer algorithms, it (supposedly) could tell the weight of the plane etc. The PURPOSE of SOME of the radars was to "discriminate" between REAL incoming warhead, and the dummy warheads that we thought the "enemy" would also send up as decoys. Bottom line – the radars, along with the computers behind them, could do some pretty amazing things in terms of tracking and identifying misiles – incoming and outgoing.

Bob Barclay I figure if one party tows the radioactive remains of a death dealing machine into another party's lagoon, then that second party can put all the graffiti they want on it! Better yet, paint the whole thing pink and put daisies on it.

Jerry Fishback Any mention in these posts of mischief night? Only place I ever heard of mischief night. Cases of shaving cream at the teen center, and fire extinguisher-launched eggs! The latter was not condoned, of course.

Tom Daly Yea the Yuk movie was for adults only and as soon as the lights went out the kids would sneak in. It was part of the Kwaj experience

Donna Miller I remember swimming to and from the doc left of the lagoon and hoping the sharks didn't eat me. I remember the healing power of the ocean and the love and support extended to me and my family. I remember falling in love. I remember...

Marilyn Hall Baysek I can't remember our maid's name, but she had very few teeth, ironed (squatting, Marshalese-style) with the board totally on the floor, and taught me to snap my gum, a "talent" that has haunted me to this day!

Stephan Calar We never had a maid but i swear every one of them came by our trailer on their way to the Tarlang to buy fish from us. We lived next to the bike racks at Echo pier and on payday Fridays I'd hear "boy, you get fish?" outside our door. Kept my brothers and me busy. I want that job back...

Bob Swanson 4th hole had the beer machine, 5th went around the ammo dump, 6th when down further and 7 & 8 were the 1100 yards back to the 9th!

Rod Hepburn Easiest was having one of your 'friends' that worked at Surfway load 4 cases on a taxi and have them delivered right to your house and stashed under your bed.

Karen Haugen Davis Oh yes, I was on crutches after my steel wire brush scrape out for my coral infection, only to need the crutches shortly after when I hit a little island man on my bike and broke my foot!!

Susan Remick Drout I had blood poisoning in my foot up into my leg from coral infection....gosh, I had a bandage and I had to wear flip-flops for a few weeks...ugh...

Rod Hepburn In a nutshell... the little boy decided that he didn't like me and got a kitchen knife. Then he 'threatened' me (kid was mebbe 4 or 5) and I had to figger how to defuse the situation. I told him I'd call Santa Claus but he didn't drop the knife. So I picked up the fone and showed him as I dialed, S – A – N – and then he started to cry and put the knife back on the counter. Probably should've left the house (trailer?) and called the cops but I was already on my 2nd beer or so.... Pretty sure I didn't babysit much after that, convinced my folks that I'd spend my time better (and more profitable) fishing at night at the pier and selling my catch to the Marshallese. Don't remember the kids' name, who knows, might be on this list now?? Year was '67 or '68

The Friends of KWAJ

Kim Klein, Michael Bayouth, Rick Medeiros, Barbara Adent Linares, Ron Bickford, Steve Espinosa, Laurie Sherman, Christy Vento Perkins, Sonya Haugen, Kwaj Podge, Johnt Keeling, Bob Swanson, Susan Remick Drout, Janette Waddell, Joan Funk, Cindy Chan, Kristi Jaekel Wilfong, Cindi Benn Evans, Noelani Kalahiki Butler, Pamela Espinosa, Sandra Hickey, Dan Kain, Rod Hepburn, Nick Keller, Clifford Cosbodillo, Paul Nappe, Lisa Kobayashi, Michael Roberts, Brian Buckley, Deborah L. Keith, Alan David Gould, Vicki Vann Pack, Carrie Hughes Shaw, Korri Brown, Karen Haugen Davis, David Espinosa, Mona Vento James, Bill Remick, Keith Kolischak, Gary Cuesta, Cathy Foote McCoil, Meleah Bauman, Patrick W. Caskey, Craig Hergenrother, Cynthia Messervy Pederson, Phil Nader, Al Catoggio, Calvin Charles Curtis Jr., Lori Fiester, Shermie Wiehe, Jay Hewitt, David Gaffny, Will Wagner, Misty Meyers, Warren Ching, Scott Johnson, Lauren Buck Medeiros, Robert M Bowman, Christine Mayhan Ecker, Karen Keller Floor, Melissa Butler, Ingrid Calar, Tom Turner, Donna Miller, Kevin Harding, Pam Lewis, Rosemary Cameron, Claire Brown Stepleton, Colleen Maxwell, Joe Bauman, Wendy Smith Powers, Marla Timas Hinojos, Karen L Painter, Brenna Mathiasen, Cheryl Anne Hine Barber, Lauren Wingate Kantz, Ronell Kuratsu von Chance-Stutler, Leslie Norris, Phil Hood, Kathy Copes Pershing, Bonny Woodford, Jerri Ellen Brewer- Greagrey, Teresa Withers, Emil Eastburn, Jerry Freeryah, Dave Tanner, Borden Black, Terry Hill Stengel, Tom Karch, Robin S. Ireland, Scott Carpenter, Beverly Barclay, Elaine VanNortwick Snyder, Candi Nissim, Kathy Loeb Williamson, Rosalinda Johnson, Tom Burkhalter, Brian Gough, Kevin Koppenhaver, Judy Fiske, Ron M. Miller, Donna Beach Williams, Ken Colburn, Fred Clark, Tony Popovich, Cheryl Sabiston Arnette, Lynne Perryman Sniffen, Lisa Buck Haley, Nadine Morgan, Cheryl Ostrander, Rob Weinberg, Shannon Hoppes Mapes, Mark Sharpe, Kenneth Zarnoch, Charlene Chisholm Taylor, Ron Chisholm, Jeffrey J Zarnoch, Patti Moore, Marlene Schimmelfennig, Kay Anson Clayton, Linda Mitchell, Barbara Allen, Jeralee Gonzalez, Wayne Marhefka, Jenny Specker, Ron Tanner, Craig Britton, Dave Zarnoch, Joe Mayhan Jr., Barbara Binger Arace, Inez Korff, Jonezy Joseph Melroy, Russ Larson, Rex A. Simmons, Scott Gramos, Brian Barna, Lee Ann Meyers Stone, Margot Mackey, Megan Stegmann Moore, Rebekah Radisch, Sam Suppe, Stan Jazwinski, Vincent Cardillo, John Sorensen, Michael Buckley, Chris Amador, Peter Iaros, Kate Endres Bauer, Debi Radisch, Chris Russell, David Baysinger, Janet Kelley, Cec Detchemendy Gillihan, Janet Rossi, Robert Sadler, John Gray, Jim Kendrick, Kenneth Adair, Julie Hileman, Eric George, Julianne Kirchner, John Merrill, Danna Dihel Lau, Reveille Patterson, Kristi Slater Sisk, Martin Ramirez, Emily James Barkley, Lynn L Dargie, Shari Winkler Allen, John "Johny" Thomason, Jeanne Baysinger Wallace, Kathy Armstrong Nelson, Mike Green, Omar D. Crafton, Doug Carr, Kenny Davis, Christie Allen Hall, Patricia Coon Parrish, Kip Correnti, Mary Georgesen, Craig Bechtold, Joe Burke, Catherine Moir Duncan, Roberta Colucci, Brent Maas, Nancy Thorpe, Lynda Rice Engels, Glenn Schwesinger, Gail Mulder Rossman, Debra Tyler, Katy Allen Jones, Linda Whitehead, Eric George, Julie Hileman, Craig Britton, Dave Zarnoch, Joyce Satermo Leigh, Rose Wilkinson, Kim Zarnoch Santone, Stephan Calar, J.P. Corey, Chuck Colburn, Raina Weyen, Jackie Vise Dingler, Tom Daly, Ned Roberts, Lisa Nelson Hendricks, Yvonne Jackson, Paul McGrew, Bill Kievenaar, Lothar Cramer, Peggy Blake, Tracy Allen Sacco, Debbie Dunagan Underwood, Art Kilo, Mike Nappe, Patty Jimenez, Rob Mount, Jayne Caskey Mack, Caroline Morton Brown, Rebecca Mounce Perrenot, Karen Petersen, Vicki Schmersahl, Laura Christensen, Barbara Logan, Heidi Owens, Dianne Waddell Michels, Michael Schultz, Diane Fellhoelter Plocher, Lisa Kennemer Dawson, Pam Putman Nodland, Dottie Healy, Yowke Net, Brandt Schmersahl, Michael E. Hasler, Diana Kyle, Susan Kea Newkirk, Tricia Anne Boswell, Joan Kalahiki, Carl Christensen, Lynn T. Edwards, George Gunther, Judy Nichols Van Wilpe, Candace Brown, Linda Catoggio, Scott Munzig, Craig Britton, John A. Phillips IV, Dottie Healy, Sheila Belarmino Brock, Dale Anson, Shannon Stein Ericsson, Julia Sorenson Porter, Lynde Molloy, Melanie Herring Gonzales, Doug Sims, Steve Nappe, Kev Sullivan, David Johnson, Jill Gjertson Brown, Jennifer Susie Burns, Dwight Barna, Sally Gould, Kevin Allas, Delia Coble-Garrison, Jim Fulp, Oliver Forest McKinney, Marie Harrell, Rick Foote, Mark Tietz, Dick Buckley, Harold Gene Doles, Nathan A. Bartlett, John Tapia, Glenn Miller, John Tapia, Lydia Menzies, Krista Haugen, Doug Slater, Thomas Stilwell, Francis Calar, Susan Blair Hensley, Kim Sullivan Farnham, Tom Eastman, Judy Sullivan Demaree, DeeDee Moseley Kennicutt, Jody Ragan Taylor, Raun Kupiec, Steve Metzner, Bret Bechtold, Jay Stepleton, Bill Moseley, Christopher Tietz, John Burney, Mark Sahl, Ronald Brophy, Dru Foster Hites, Cynthia Terwilliger, Debbie Kessler, Vicki Addy Ryan, Bob Dagling, Therese M. Picado, Bog Scanoll, Joanne Garland, Jennifer Brooks, Collette Warren George, Manny Casipit, Bill and Dayna Beavers, Georgette Pizzio, Mark Blair, Gretchen Almond, Elle May Moore, Dearing Railroad, Paul Kniatt, Janie Schroer Manley, Jeff Edwards, Sheila Gold, Mary M. Van Houten, Betty Bowman Urick, Kathleen Inglis, Wanda Smith Mannahan, Fred Hodde, Kim Kaholokula Waters, Wendy Wood, Chris Hergenrother Ford, Bahar Malia Porter Otken, Kathy L Sawyer, Kelly Thurber Starek, Deborah Kramer Valentine, Kelly Taylor Counts, Cliff Geyer, Helene Suzanne Phileger, Erika Vee Dubb, Betsy Spencer Gandara Bruinsma, Lisa Fiske Schrimsher, Jeananne Phillips Jackson, Jeanne Bliss, Dan Derbawka, Steven Lee, Donna Moseley Connors, Leslie Mount Frieder, Valerie Menice Chapman, Jim Rhea, Frank Serafini Sr., Cathy A Hughes-Elliott, Bob Parks, Robert Rhea, Gerry Crossman, Bonny Specker, Bill Stepchew, Julie Hergenrother Tanner, C. V. Keeling, Diane Hodson, Eric Keoni Duarte, Jeff Marsh, Kathy Wirt Bradway, Ed Ice, Anuhea Kalahiki Maurer, Tom Zebal, Laura Graham-Marquard, Cordes Finger, Pamela Hashemi-Blake, Elise Burt, Jack Bartholomew, Jetta McDonald, Gayle Roberts Sklar, Phyllis Anson, Christine Quackenbush-Carey, Norma Jean Williams, Julia Compoc, Sandy Castle, Kate James Bernsen, Renee Bevard, David Angell, Julie Anne Beer, Sonja Hansell Olsen, Bob Barclay, Samuel Ice, Vanessa Ronetz, Janice Bartlett O'Brien, Mikelle K. Lucero, Dean Haugen, Jo Gjertson Frederiksen, Linda Narleski Ruth, Heidi Calar Barfield, Alice Cuba, Jeff Fox, Nancy Burton Deal, Sam Miller, Jerry Fishback, Mike Detchemendy, Susan Bernella Herring, Dave Blackwell, Panida Lachman, Eddie Hosmer, Nancy Nelson Warren, Keith Matthews, Mike Wilson, Detchemendy Mark, Lois Tom McArthur, Kai Kalahiki, JoAnne Christensen, Susan Kay Perkins Knudson, Dwight Ross, Sheri Courtney, Armand Conan LaPointe, Kirk Searle, Craig Koller, Carl Berndtson, Jennifer Salhus, Karen Wingate Campbell, Mark Kaholokula, Leslie Kirkham, Keith Allas, Larry Brantley, Peyton Monroe, Gary Stenvers, Cherie Rodecker Groll, Andy Standen, Donna Harrison Burch, Jody Ragan Taylor, Marilyn Hall Baysek, Shana Kuratsu, Stan Roberts, Christopher Barna, Michael Brzoznowski, Kim Koller Walker, Don Stapleton, Lonnie Sykos, Bill Allen, Alan Taylor, Terry Fisher, Kevin Brewer, Ann Deals, Patty May Swigart, Tiffani Villa, Bob Willingham, Brenda Sweetland Jackson Brewer, Karen Christensen Free, Linda Webb, Dana Lucero, Catherine Crash Castelli Persello, Holly Wylie Sanchez, Sharen Cutler Sherman EA, Andrea Maitra, Michael Rauchwerk, Patty Poop, Clara Medeiros, Mary Kay Vuksanovich, Nancy Garcia-Ganan, Cory Campbell, Alma Lorenz, Charles Serafini, Fran Gouveia Swehla, Susan Gould, Felicia Baker, Steven Robbins, Bill Moseley, Iwalani Carr, Joseph Benn, Mary Kay Ley, Cort Weaver, Joann Brogden Condrey, Ronnie Loporcaro, Robert Kirkland, Laura Gudzikowski Jacobs, Andrea McManus, Debra Patton, Becky Cuba, Abigail Caro, Jerry Cuesta, Jim Keenan, Jerry Cuba, Cheryl Cuba-May, Rodney Karch, Claudia Marapoti Gill, Candace Hergenrother, John Walter Fiske, Kammy Ragan Minor, Sandi Moseley Hult, Stacy VanPelt Zarnoch, Betsy Hall, Maylene Bird, Linda Gruebner

For more information about *Nine Degrees North*, the novel,
please contact Palm Avenue Publishing:
www.sonofjason.com/contact

For information, updates and offers on all Palm Avenue
Publishing projects, sign up on our mailing list at
www.sonofjason.com/project2
www.facebook.com/NineDegreesNorth